PAINTED EARTH TEMPLE

THE
WHITE BUFFALO WOMAN
TRILOGY

PAINTED
EARTH TEMPLE
BOOK TWO

HEYOKA MERRIFIELD

ATRIA BOOKS
New York London Toronto Sydney

BEYOND WORDS
PUBLISHING

ATRIA BOOKS
1230 Avenue of the Americas
New York, NY 10020

BEYOND WORDS
PUBLISHING
20827 N.W. Cornell Road, Suite 500
Hillsboro, Oregon 97124-9808
503-531-8700 – 503-531-8773 fax
www.beyondword.com

Copyright © 2002, 2007 by Heyoka Merrifield

The information contained in this book is intended to be educational. The author and publisher are in no way liable for any misuse of the information.

Managing editor: Henry Covi
Proofreaders: Meadowlark Communications, Inc.
Cover design: Carol Sibley
Composition: William H. Brunson Typography Services
Interior artwork: Heyoka Merrifield
Cover and Epilogue artwork: Keith Powell

Library of Congress Cataloging-in-Publication Data

Merrifield, Heyoehkah, 1940–
    Painted earth temple: book two of The White Buffalo Woman trilogy/
by Heyoka Merrifield. — 1st Atria books/Beyond Words hardcover ed.
    p. cm. — (White Buffalo Woman trilogy; bk. 2)
    Originally published: Rainbird Publishers, © 2002.
    1. Paleolithic period—Europe—Fiction. I. Title.
    PS3563.E7445P35   2006
    813′.54—dc22
                                                    2006029714
ISBN-13: 978-1-58270-152-3
ISBN-10:   1-58270-152-0

First Atria Books/Beyond Words trade paperback edition March 2007

10 9 8 7 6 5 4 3 2 1

ATRIA BOOKS is a trademark of Simon & Schuster, Inc.

Beyond Words Publishing is a division of Simon & Schuster, Inc.

Manufactured in the United States of America

For more information about special discounts for bulk purchases, please contact Simon & Schuster Special Sales at 1-800-456-6798 or business@simonandschuster.com.

The corporate mission of Beyond Words Publishing, Inc.: *Inspire to Integrity*

Dedication

I dedicate *Painted Earth Temple* to my friend and
medicine brother George Harrison, for he joined the
world of spirit as the last few chapters were being
written. George was a calm center in the hurricane
of misplaced archetypal mythic images with which
our society seems to resonate. Living in this most
difficult environment, he was able to find peace
while striving to walk in balance and embracing life
as a quest for spiritual understanding. Although our
paths on this quest differed, our hearts understood
that the path is really only one.

As I write this dedication, an eagle flies past my
window toward the mountains, disappearing into
the west. In the ancient Earth traditions, this is
seen as a gift from the Sacred Powers and it tells
me that my friend is close by. May his spirit always
soar with the eagles.

Contents

Prologue

From my earliest memories, ceremony has always stimulated a beautiful part of myself. Something spoke to my heart during the communion ritual in my father's church, the decorating of the Christmas tree, and the carving of Jack-o-lanterns at Halloween. I see all parts of our ceremonial life as gifts from our ancient ancestors. In my art and in my life I have explored the power in these ancient treasures. Honoring the genetic memory of my Native American heritage, I now dance in the yearly healing sundance and pray frequently in the purifying heat of the sweatlodge. And I explore whenever possible remnants of the myths and ceremonies of our other ancestors from around the world.

I feel that our Paleolithic Grandparents made every aspect of their lives a ceremony of celebration, and I also aspire to do so in my life. I do not know exactly what kind of ceremonies took place in their beautifully painted caves, some of which I have had the good fortune to visit. Even so, as I entered these silent, ancient temples I felt my ceremonial heritage awaken.

I offer this book from a place within me that loves ceremony and from which it has become deeply woven into my life. I hope that it may begin to provide a better understanding of our grandparents and our spiritual heritage than the scientific approach taken by most of our current-day anthropologists.

The story of Painted Earth Temple springs from the way I imagine our hunting and gathering ancestors lived before, and for a few ages after, the great Earth changes of 11,500 years ago. The story takes place around 3,600 years ago when the world shook with the eruption of Mt. Thera in the Mediterranean Sea, the largest volcanic eruption in recorded history. This heralded a period of increased climatic change, occurring at a time when our Aryan ancestors began to overwhelm the older cultures of the world. The People of the Painted Earth Temple were some of the last surviving hunter-gatherers in Europe. Their small village, nestled in a hidden valley in the Alps, was separated from the nearest neighboring tribe by several weeks' journey over treacherous trails.

Acknowledgments

I would like to thank the many friends who have helped me, encouraged me, and made editorial suggestions during the writing of this book. Among them are Keith Powell, Sandy Valenzano, Terrill Croghan, Kathy Smick, Maquel Ames, Katherine Straus, Harry Strunk, Snow Deer, Barbara Clow, and the staff at Beyond Words Publishing and Atria Books.

In celebration of
All My Relations

The Great Web of Time

Each year, the sun travels along its ecliptic path through the twelve constellations of the zodiac; it journeys through the Four Corners of the Sky House: the spring equinox, the summer solstice, the autumn equinox, and the winter solstice. There is also a slow wobbling of the Earth's axis that causes the precession of the equinoxes. This precession is usually called the Platonic Year or the Great Year and it is about 26,000 years long. Visualize a large circle in the night sky above the Earth with the North Star, Polaris, on it. As the North Pole moves along the circle, other stars will become the North Star, until after 26,000 years Polaris will again point to the north. This also causes a new zodiac constellation to be on the horizon as the sun rises during the equinox about every 2,000 years. We are at this time, passing from the Age of Pisces into the Age of Aquarius. The Vedic astronomers, the Egyptians, the Greeks, the Mayans, and many other of our ancestors held the precession as a sacred cosmic event. I include the drawing on the next page to show when the People of the Painted Earth Temple lived on this Great Wheel of Time.

The Great Web of Time

(Showing the approximate dates of major events of the Platonic Year.)

1   35,500 BC to 9500 BC. The Golden Age of the Goddess (Paleolithic Age) is the period before the Earth's near-collision with another celestial body that caused the Earth's axis to tilt and wobble.

2   9500 BC. The time of cataclysmic Earth changes. Atlantis and other lands sink into the oceans while the Himalayas and other mountains rise. The changes are marked by the creation of the Sphinx during the Age of Leo.

3   5600 BC. The Black Sea flood, which is the origin of the biblical story of the Great Flood. This caused the dislocation of the civilizations between the Mediterranean Sea and the Black Sea.

4   3500 BC. In the Sahara, river and lake systems dry up and the Egyptians return to the Nile Valley. Toward the end of the Age of Taurus, the Old Kingdom in Egypt is called the Pyramid Age.

5   1630 BC. Thera (now called the island of Sentorini) erupts, the largest volcanic eruption in recorded history, causing weather changes and the dislocation of many tribes. This is the period when the story of the Painted Earth Temple takes place.

6   Zero Point. The Age of Pisces begins around the time of the birth of Jesus Christ.

7   AD 2012. The end of the Mayan calendar, which differs slightly from the Platonic calendar. This date also marks the beginning of the Mayan full precessional cycle of 25,626 years. Around this time is the beginning of the Age of Aquarius, our present place on this Wheel of Time.

The Web of Life

The People of the Painted Earth Temple lay sleeping in the early morning. Spotted Cat awakened before twilight and rolled up his sleeping skins, tying them together with a thong. He stuffed a bundle of dried meat into his bedding and slipped quietly out of the circle of thatched lodges.

Cat was not doing anything wrong, but he had not shared with anyone his plan to climb to the top of the Sacred Mountain. The young men of the tribe climbed the mountain as part of their initiation. Also known as White Mountain, it stood like a guardian over the valley that the People called the Nest. Snow covered the mountain's pointed peak all year and three creeks flowed down from it.

The center of these flowed over a high waterfall that connected the mountain and the valley.

Although no one had forbidden Cat to climb White Mountain, several cycles of seasons would pass before his initiation ceremony, and the tribal elders might not approve of a boy of seven winters spending a night alone there. But something was stirring in him, and he felt a need for adventure.

The summer heat made climbing more difficult than Cat had foreseen, and the bundle on his back made his shoulders throb. He stopped often to drink from a nearby rushing stream, a gift from the snow lingering on the mountaintop. As he rose from the bank of the stream, wiping his face, something in a tree on the opposite bank caught his attention.

A large antelope carcass lay draped over the fork of the tree. He had never seen such a thing before and wondered how the animal had come to die in a tree. As Cat tried to understand this puzzle, he realized that another pair of eyes followed him, behind them a presence trying to understand the sight of this young two-legged creature by the stream. Chills crept up Cat's back to his head, making the small hairs on his neck rise. In the shadows among the leaves, a huge shape came into focus. A large snow leopard relaxed there, her legs dangling on either side of a limb, her eyelids drooping halfway down her yellow eyes. The great feline sleepily shut them to continue her full-bellied nap in the summer heat.

Spotted Cat rose slowly and quietly took a few steps backward. The leopard's eyes snapped open. As he and the leopard locked in eye-to-eye contact, Spotted Cat realized that this was the first time he had seen his guiding animal spirit and namesake. He had never heard of a snow leopard attacking any of the People, so his fear receded a bit.

It seemed to Cat that the animal was trying to communicate something to him. Her eyes broke contact with his and looked down at Spotted Cat's feet. As he looked too, he could see that he stood where the antelope had been killed. Among the bloodstained rocks at his feet, an ivory-colored object drew his attention. One of the leopard's claws had been broken off in the struggle with the great antelope. He realized at once that the leopard had made a give-away to him. Cat had always wanted a token from his medicine animal, like many of the People wore. He thanked the snow leopard for the power gift and left a piece of dried meat as an offering where he had found the claw.

Spotted Cat started walking very slowly away from the stream. He took a few steps and wondered if the snow leopard was following him. Turning around, Cat saw that she was still in the tree gazing at him. A wave of warmth seemed to flow into Cat's heart from his medicine animal's power. He continued walking, although after a few more steps he had to turn and look at her one last time. The leopard had disappeared, and for the remainder of Cat's walk up the mountain, he felt her presence near him.

The last part of the long hike in the smoldering summer day was the steepest and most difficult. Cat arrived exhausted at a lake that reflected White Mountain on its surface. He dove into the cool water and felt the healing water spirits take the fatigue from his muscles. After emerging from the water, Cat realized that he could go no farther this day and he gathered a bundle of sticks for a campfire.

As he sat by his fire, Cat fashioned a new thong by braiding four strips of hide together as Grandmother Spider Woman had taught him. He attached the leopard claw to the thong and put it around his neck. A power surrounded his body that felt similar to the radiance that seemed to encircle the snow leopard. He felt no fear as he lay wrapped in his sleeping skins and stared in wonder at the stars.

Spotted Cat awoke at first light and gazed dreamily at the morning sky. An intricate spider web stretched between two trees near where he lay. It was covered with dewdrops and the sun shining on the web created a rainbow that glowed upon it. Shivers ran over his skin as he thought about sleeping so close to a spider. Cat always felt squeamish whenever he found himself near a creepy crawler.

Spotted Cat picked up his bundle of sleeping skins and started down the animal trail that ran beside the stream. He was anxious to show Grandmother the gift talisman from his animal power. Cat noticed that he was the first creature to walk along the trail that day, for there were no prints on the dew-covered path. With his head bent over looking for a sign, he walked right into a huge spider web.

Thinking of how large the spider that made this web must be sent a jolt through his body. He quickly brushed the tickling, sticky fibers from his face and combed his fingers through his hair to make sure the spider was not on his head. Cat felt ashamed to fear this small creature that was also the power animal of his Grandmother.

To confront his fear and find his way through it, Cat resolved to walk the untrodden trail and pay no attention to any webs. Every few steps, another web stretched across the trail. Since he was walking naked in the mild summer morning, his entire body soon tingled with an array of spider webs. He became aware of every sensation on the surface of his skin. Cat also began to sense how the strands of spider web connected him to the trees, shrubs, flowers, and rocks that he passed. The feeling of connection with his surroundings increased until he seemed to become a part of everything along the trail.

Cat saw deer tracks enter the trail and the spider webs across the path ended. His joining with his environment now expanded to include the deer and all the creatures of the forest. He remained in this altered awareness, feeling the totality of his surroundings and his oneness with it, for the rest of his walk back to the village.

Spotted Cat arrived at the village and found Grandmother Spider Woman weaving a basket decorated with butterfly designs. These small baskets were the type that the women liked to wear as hats. Grandmother's huge size always amazed Cat. Although she was a short woman, she weighed twice as much as any other woman in the tribe. She was the tribe's High Priestess and represented Gaia, the Goddess of the Land.

Grandmother held the power of the Earth Mother for the People of the Painted Earth Temple. When hunters returned from a hunt they always gave an offering of the best part of the animal to Spider Woman. The High Priestess ate the offering, symbolizing the completion of the ceremonial circle of the animal's give-away. The life of the animal went back to the Mother Earth. The spirit of the animal then felt appreciated and honored, and encouraged to return. The reborn animal could then give-away to the People again.

A similar token was given to Grandmother when the People gathered roots, seeds, fruit, and herbs. Over the many winters that Spider Woman had been High Priestess, she had grown to an enormous size. Her voluminous breasts and her round pregnant-like belly symbolized the abundance of the Earth and the prosperity of the tribe.

When the hunters and gatherers were away from the village for days at a time, a small carving of the Gaia Goddess traveled with them. They placed this small ivory statue on the ground by the hearth fire and fed to the fire spirits the offerings to Mother Earth. Like Spider Woman, the Gaia carvings had large, round breasts and bellies.

While Spider Woman sat weaving the beautiful design with her nimble fingers, Cat told her of his White Mountain adventure. She sat quiet for a while as several layers of grasses danced around the small basket, then said:

"What happened to you on this journey is big medicine. It has brought you closer to your initiation time and has affirmed my intuition concerning the identity of your power animal, the snow leopard.

The teaching that the spider medicine gave to you is a wonderful gift. The rainbow that you awoke to is a reflection of the medicine power of light. Although light is white, when it joins with rain, waterfalls, or dewdrops, the rainbow magic is created. The one white light becomes the six colors within the rainbow. Likewise, there is light energy within the Earth, and it enters our feet and rises upward. This light also turns into the colors of the rainbow.

Our bodies have seven moving circles of light within them. The lowest circle is in the seeds-of-creation center. The color of this circle is red. The second circle of light is orange and is where food is changed into life's essence. The source of life's breath is at the third circle and its color is yellow. At the heart power center, the fourth circle is green. The fifth circle is blue and radiates from the throat. At the brow, the sixth circle is purple. The seventh circle of light is at the top of the head and the light here is white.

Each circle of light has an animal's medicine power. The first circle has the medicine power of the snake. Some of the snake's gifts are the physical body, pleasure, pain, and creativity. Fish are always in motion through water and they are the animals of the second circle. This movement reflects the feeling awareness that is the power of the fish. The third, yellow circle of light is the power of mind that can take flight like its animal, the bird. The animals of the fourth circle nurse their children with milk. The loving and nurturing that these animals show their young comes from the power of the heart circle. At the throat center is the human animal. The power here is speech. The power of all these circles finally gathers within the forehead. When we open this circle of light we can see into the world of Spirit. At the top of the head, the many colors become a single white light, connecting us with the All That Is. Light enters from the Sky through this seventh circle of light. The Sky's light is equal in power to the light from the Earth, and when they join in the heart they dance the Sacred Balance.

All these moving circles create a body of light that surrounds our physical bodies. This light body is woven by and reflects the seven circles. The different colors are like a painting of light that tells a story to a healer about how best to heal a body's sickness. As you become a healer, you will learn to see this body of light and you will learn what the various colors mean."

Grandmother placed the now-finished woven basket in Spotted Cat's hands, and he turned it over and admired the intricate designs as she continued:

"What you felt as you walked along the path is called the Web of Life. Everything surrounding us seems to be separate, but all is connected like a spider web stretched across the All That Is. Where the strands cross and touch, there is a tree, a rock, a human, a star, or some other being. Whatever affects any one of these beings affects the whole Web. The medicine power that came to you affected me and our tribe and sent vibrations throughout the entire Web, even to the stars.

You came into the Web of Life with the helping power of a spotted cat, the snow leopard. This power will influence your gifts in life. You are not a herd creature. You are a solitary creature and will enjoy roaming far from our tribal circle. Where many of our tribe feel very uncomfortable away from the community of the People, you feel joy in your wandering, the same as your medicine animal.

The place on the Web of Life into which an individual is woven determines his place on the Path of Fate. Fate opens before us our life's journey, but it does not determine how we use our gifts of power. We may cause very little disturbance in the Web of Life or we may develop all of our gifts of power until we help cause a shift in the entire Web. I have chosen you along with a village girl close to your age, White Bison Calf, to be my apprentices. The reason I have picked you both is that I feel that you will honor, celebrate, and develop your gifts of power."

Cat felt a bit overwhelmed by all this information given to him by Grandmother Spider Woman, yet he also felt its resonance within his body in a way he could not fully grasp. He knew too that, above all else, he had been honored by Grandmother choosing him to be her apprentice, and that somehow his life had changed when she imparted her wisdom to him.

The Story of Creation

few winters after Spotted Cat's Sacred
Mountain adventure, he walked with his
friend, White Bison Calf, to the night fire
in the center of the village. The People were joy-
ously drumming and singing. After the music came
to an end, someone asked Grandfather Tree Spirit
to tell a story. Calf chimed in, "Grandfather, tell
the story of how the first people came to be on
the Earth."

Everyone fell silent as the old shaman began
to speak:

"Before any creature existed, there was
only the sacred silence that we call Sky

Mother or the Sacred Void. Her body was a dark void and this darkness was the All That Is. Our dark mother had a thought: I would like to create another being. When Sky Mother had this thought, a bolt of lightning pierced the Sacred Void, causing a clap of thunder. This first sound was the loudest sound ever made. The bolt of lightning and thunder became Sky Father.

Sky Mother was very excited by her creation and her excitement caused sparks to scatter from the lightning bolt. The many sparks became the stars and the bolt's journey through the Sacred Darkness became the path of the spirit world. We can look up now and see this path of stars reaching across the sky."

Everyone gazed at the stars, thinking about Sky Father's journey through the blackness of night. All eyes were again on Tree as he continued:

"Now, Sky Father became excited about his part in creating the stars and he reached out to Sky Mother and they embraced. The Sacred Twins of Creation were happy to have someone to reflect themselves. Their exhilaration caused the stars to give birth to the many worlds so they would have companions.

The worlds birthed by the stars were cold and dark like huge black boulders, larger than many mountains. The lightning bolt hurtled through the blackness, surrounded by the stars and their children worlds. While still in an embrace, Mother and Father Sky felt like they were merging into one being when they collided with the world we walk on. The impact caused them to tingle with rapture and heightened their sense of unity. The Sacred Twins of Creation felt the ecstasy of joining, and all of Earth's creatures came into being. There were two of every creature, so they too would have someone to reflect themselves.

Sky Mother and Sky Father were so astounded by their creations that they hovered above the Earth in wonder. Sky Father was reflected through the sun and Sky Mother was reflected through the moon. At this time, there was no death or birth on Earth, and no one had to eat food or drink water to stay alive. All of the first creatures could communicate with each other and understood that they were related and had the same parents.

After a while, the First Man and the First Woman on Earth thought they would like to have children because it would be good to feel the joy of creating new life and to have more reflections of themselves. First Woman and Man called a council meeting with a male and female representative of each group of beings. Sitting in this council circle with First Woman and First Man were the families of Mammoth for the four-legged, Crow for the winged, Spider for the creepy crawlers, Whale for the water people, Oak Tree for the growing people, Snake for the wisdom people, and White Crystal for the stone people. All the creatures in the council liked the idea of creating beings like themselves to be their children.

Oak Mother said to the circle, 'So we may have the ability of creation, we need to have medicine power from our parents.'

White Crystal Mother suggested, 'Since Crow Mother and Crow Father can fly, let us send them to the moon and sun for the medicine that we need.'

The Crows flew off, one to the sun and one to the moon. Crow Mother took a big bite from the moon and the council saw the crescent moon and knew that Crow Mother had succeeded. Crow Father flew to the sun to take a bite, but the sun was so hot that his feathers caught fire. Burning and leaving a trail of smoke, Crow Father fell to Earth. At the last moment, he spread his wings and landed with his tail feathers still on fire. The bush that he landed on started burning and this was the first time that the world had the gift of the fire spirits. Crow Father jumped down to the ground and sat in a stream to put out the fire in his tail. Then the Crows sat back down in the council circle."

The fire in the middle of the gathered villagers cracked loudly, sending a billowing spiral of sparks toward the stars. The People of the Painted Earth Temple raised their hands toward the fire, then patted their bodies with this blessing. They were thankful that the fire spirits, gifted to the People by Crow Father, had spoken to them this night. Then their storyteller continued:

"Snake Father spoke next: 'It was the idea of First Woman and First Man to create children and have this council meeting. I think they should be the first to merge with the moon and sun.'

17

First Woman took a piece of moon and ate it. In this ceremony, time was created by the cycles of the moon. First Woman's body was marked by the moon cycles growing to full and then back to new. Then First Man ate some of the fire from the burning bush. Next, all of Earth's creatures took turns eating part of the sun and moon. When they had eaten the medicine power of their parents, everyone returned to their lodges and made love medicine to begin creating children.

After First Woman had eaten the medicine of the moon, she received the earth wisdom of Mother Gaia and the feeling awareness of Mother Moon. With this wisdom, First Woman knew that she had become the first Priestess and that she must be a teacher to the children who would come from her. As the Priestess, First Woman realized that she would represent the Mother Earth to the People.

In order for all creatures to remember that they were related to Sky Mother and Sky Father, First Woman asked Spider Mother to teach her how to weave. Spider Mother taught her this skill and then the Priestess wove the first basket. Using medicine energy, she then wove a luminous web. First, she wove two threads to make the Sacred Cross and join the Powers of the Four Directions. Then she wove a spiral of energy that touched all of Earth and Sky's creatures so they would always be connected in the Web of Life.

After her weaving, First Woman began to feel new life in her body and the need to nourish herself by eating food. She took the fruit of the apple tree and ate it to give life to the growing baby in her womb. This apple was the first death in the world. She then gave the seeds back to the earth to grow more trees.

First Man received the wisdom of the creative mind when he ate the fire, and he understood that he could make tools for hunting animals. Observing the deer tribe, he saw that the herd would soon become food for the People. He also saw how protective Deer Father was of Deer Mother. Like the King Stag, First Man felt that he should create a circle of protection around First Woman. The closer she approached her time of birthing, the more help and security she needed. By offering this supportive power, First Man realized he had become the First Horned Shaman. He would hold the power of the Earth Father for the humans. He was to be a healer to the People, protector of the Priestess, and a teacher of the Sacred Balance.

First Man also felt the need to eat to keep the fire of creation burning in his body. To feed the fire within him, First Man caught Fish Father and ate him. This was the first death of an animal. Fish Father had mated with Fish Mother and she had many fish children that carried on the life of the fish tribe.

In order for birth to happen, death had to happen. Death was not an ending; it brought birth and a new beginning. At the moment of death, the spirit of a creature would always return to the One Spirit to be recreated in the Circle of Life.

The first crows were all white, yet when they had crow children, they were black from Crow Father's burnt feathers. When the first crows touched the Sacred Twins of Creation, they learned about the sacred laws. They could see into the past, present, and future. Crows became the medicine power guiding us to understand that the past is our teacher, the present is our creation, and the future is our vision. Ever since this flight, when they brought the moon cycles and the creative light down to Earth, crows have been seen as the law birds of time and space."

After hearing this story the villagers sat in silence, gazing at the glowing coals of the night fire. In the pale orange light cast by the flames, Calf saw all of the creatures in the creation story sitting in places of honor around Tree Spirit.

The Initiation of White Bison Calf

It was the autumn of White Bison Calf's thirteenth winter and her body was feeling strange. She decided that she would go to Grandmother Spider Woman the next day to get healing herbs for the illness she felt. The next morning, she found blood on her sleeping skins and realized that she had begun her first moon cycle. She dressed in her finest clothes to go to Grandmother's lodge.

As she walked, Calf remembered picking berries with Spider Woman when she was a small girl. Her hands were all red and she told Grandmother that it reminded her of the time she had cut her hand with a flint knife. The pain and blood flowing out of her hand were very frightening.

Grandmother answered Calf's concern with the injury by saying, "Blood flows should not always be frightening. One day you will begin your first moon cycle and then you will be a woman. It is now time for you to start helping the village women who are having their moon cycles and staying in the moonlodge circle."

Soon after this conversation, Grandmother took Calf to the moonlodge circle. This small circle of lodges was separated from the village by a short walk and the men were not allowed there. Two other small girls sat with Spider Woman as she spoke. "I am going to teach you to help in serving the women who are in the seclusion of the moonlodge. You will prepare beautiful food offerings of special meals that are nourishing during this time. Also, you will gather dried sweet grass for the women to sit and sleep upon. The grasses will absorb the flow of the moon cycle and a grandmother will later be the one to remove the grass, for the blood has a strong power. The moon cycle blood is a gift from creation and holds the power of new life. After this power has been in a woman's body, we will burn the grass and release the power back to the Circle of Life."

As she walked to Grandmother's lodge, Calf remembered all the times she had helped the other women in their moon lodge. She realized that it was now her time to be served by the village girls, the women, and the grandmothers. When Calf arrived and told Grandmother what had happened, Spider Woman gave her a loving embrace. "It is time for your initiation ceremony and we will begin the preparations now."

Three grandmothers and three young girls were called to the lodge of the High Priestess and they all walked with Calf and Spider Woman to the Painted Earth Temple. The young girls carried dried grasses and baskets of fruit and berries arranged with flowers in a beautiful pattern.

The three girls left the food and grass by the cave door and returned to the village. Carrying oil lamps, White Bison Calf and her four elders picked up the offerings and entered the dark cave. Calf felt excitement as she walked into the Painted Earth Temple for the first time. By the light of the lamps, Calf saw wondrous paintings on the walls of the cave. Many horses ran along the walls and other animals were on the ceiling. In the flickering light of the lamps, the horses seemed to be moving like animals in the dreamtime.

They walked in silence, and after a while the women came to a round chamber. A small spring-fed pool of water rested just inside the entrance, and spread before a stone altar that held a bear's skull. Paintings of many different animals covered the inside of the chamber. Calf sat in the center on the dried grass with the four grandmothers sitting around her in the positions of the four sacred directions. The Gaia Priestess, who sat in front of the altar in the direction of west, took holy water from the spring in her hand and sprinkled herself with a blessing. She then gave a water blessing to the three other grandmothers, and last to White Bison Calf.

As the water blessing touched Calf's head, Spider Woman sang her medicine song, after which she spoke:

"The magic of creation that Crow Mother brought from the moon has awakened within you. Your body now has the potential to create a child. However, because of your responsibilities as a priestess, it will be many winters before you will feel the joy of motherhood.

As a priestess of the Mother Earth, you will be one of the keepers of this temple. In another temple room is kept a burning oil lamp that represents the Fire of Creation that Crow Father brought to Earth from the sun. It is now your duty to make sure that the lamp always has oil in it so the flame will never die. In the Longest Night

Ceremony, when all the hearth fires are put out, we will rekindle all of the village fires with fire from this Sacred Flame. Also, your first lesson as a young priestess will be a demonstration of the way we create the sacred paintings that you see in the temple."

Spider Woman took out the painting tools from her medicine bundle. She started mixing her paints, then reached over and took a small amount of Calf's moon flow from the grass to mix into the paint. She began to paint on the temple's wall. Soon, Calf saw a white bison emerging out of the picture that the Gaia Priestess was creating. As Calf watched Grandmother paint, she realized that many of the skills she had learned from Spider Woman over the cycles of seasons were to help wake up her creativity. Calf knew that she would continue the tradition of temple painting as her ancestors had done.

Upon finishing her painting, the High Priestess continued, "White Bison Calf, now you may ask this circle of grandmothers any questions you have concerning your entry into womanhood."

Calf thought to herself for a moment, then asked, "Why do women go into the moonlodge during their moon cycle time and separate themselves from the tribe?"

Before the grandmother sitting in the north answered, she presented Calf with a wonderfully painted long skirt like all the priestesses wore.

"There is a lot of mystery surrounding the blood that flows from a woman during her moon cycle. If new life comes to a woman, this would be food for the child while it is growing for nine moons in her womb. A woman on her cycle has the creative medicine from Mother Sky surrounding her, which she and her tribal family must honor.

Sometimes a little extra mystery surrounding women is helpful in the dealings with the men of the tribe, but more superstitions surround moon cycle medicine than are necessary. For instance, different from what you may have heard, it is not bad to touch a man's hunting tools during this time. The most important aspect of the seclusion of the moonlodge is that it provides a time of rest from the woman's other tribal responsibilities. We need to be free to celebrate this time when our inner powers are awakened. Also, as the men and children must function without the help of the woman, the work we do is more appreciated."

Then Calf asked, "Why do we have an initiation ceremony like this?"

The Grandmother in the east gifted Calf with a woven and decorated conical hat that the priestesses wore, then answered:

> "You are making the transition from childhood to womanhood. Now that it is possible for you to be a mother, your whole view of the world will change. These changes are very confusing and certain ceremonies can help you through the life passages they represent. Initiation will help your mind align itself with what is happening in your body.
>
> There will be another ceremony when you become a wise woman. As you grow older, your body will change again and you will no longer be able to have children. This becoming a crone, or grandmother, will be another life passage. Your elders will meet with you again to honor the wonderful changes in your body and mind when this happens in the autumn time of your life."

Calf thought again for a while as she looked at the temple's walls, then asked, "Why do we have paintings of animals on the walls of our cave temple?"

The elder sitting in the south gave Calf a healer's basket containing many smaller baskets for herbs, then spoke:

"The paintings are meant to capture the radiance of the spirit within animal powers. Most of the animals pictured on the walls are the ones that we depend upon for our food. Mother Earth has given us these gifts so that we may live. The cave is also a radiant symbol of our Mother Earth. This inner room represents her womb and the tunnel is like her birthing passage. These symbols speak not only to our minds but also to a deeper part of us. They speak to us as our dreams speak to us.

The men also use the Painted Earth Temple for their initiation and other ceremonies. Often, before they go hunting, the hunters come here and pray to the spirits of the animals they will kill in the hunt."

When the grandmother in the south had finished, Spider Woman gave Calf a carved crescent moon pendant strung on ivory beads, then spoke. "White Bison Calf, we will now leave you alone and will return with more food and fresh grass during your three days and two nights of seclusion.

During your initiation ceremony this temple is your first moonlodge." As she finished speaking, she pushed a round piece of wood into the hole from which the spring poured water into the chamber's pool. The water stopped flowing and the temple became completely silent.

After the four elders left, an empty feeling gripped Calf's stomach. To take away her fear of being alone, she rested on her back and thought of the different villagers and which power animal painted on the temple walls belonged to each person. After a while, she felt better and wanted to try sitting in the dark while going deep into her body and mind. Blowing out the wick in the oil lamp, Calf sat cross-legged as Grandmother had taught her.

Like the silence, the blackness was complete, and a little frightening. It differed dramatically from the black of night with its stars and many sounds. As she overcame her fear of the darkness, Calf became aware of her breath and it slowed and became more even. Soon, a sweet feeling washed over her and she heard a sound similar to wind blowing through countless leaves. The sound seemed to come both from within her and around her. Calf felt like she was hearing the movement of creation flowing through Mother Earth and herself. She stayed in this blissful state for an unknown stretch of time. When she eventually became tired, she lay down to sleep and began to dream.

In her dream, Calf walked through a grass-covered valley, surrounded by mountains. She saw a herd of bison and walked toward them. Unafraid, Calf walked up to a young female bison calf. She merged with the calf and then she started to glow with light. The calf turned into a fully grown white bison and she continued to walk with the herd. When Calf awoke, she thanked the powers for the medicine dream and then used firestones to restart the lamp.

On the third day of her seclusion, Calf was blessing herself with water from the Sacred Spring when she heard sounds. The four grandmothers entered the temple and again took their places in a circle.

Grandmother Spider Woman spoke:

"Before we left you here for your time of seclusion, I did not speak about what you would experience during the three days. This is because what a woman feels during her time in the moonlodge is difficult to express with words. What she experiences comes not from the mind, but from the worlds of dreams and stories.

During a woman's moon cycle, the doors separating the worlds of feelings, dreams, the Sacred Void, and the First Woman are opened. There is no separation between the childless woman, the mother, and the crone. A woman may feel the wise understanding of the crone in one instant and then journey into the mind of the young woman the next.

We go into seclusion during this cycle so that we may receive the powers that are available to us. As we go through the door into the Sacred Void, we may have a greater understanding of the creation story. This is how the stories were first learned. They are as necessary to the People as food and water. Without them, the tribe would perish. The old tales often serve to describe our own inner powers and how to resolve the conflicts that can occur between our minds and our bodies. These stories help us to heal our bodies' internal conflicts much as our dreams do.

When we experience change in ourselves, the stories must change to include these new elements. Also, during this time of power, a woman can have insights into the many choices in her life as well as the many paths available to the tribe. The understandings we experience during seclusion may blossom into new stories that will bring inner healing to the village.

You should always honor your dreams, for they are one way the other worlds and your inner powers speak to you. In the moon lodge when the doorways are open, pay even more attention to the messages in your dreams. It is also a good opportunity to have a closer relationship with the goddesses of creativity. Doing your weaving or painting during seclusion may illuminate a new form or design.

As your many inner powers are awakened during your moon cycle, they may trigger different physical body sensations. These sensations are the consciousness of creation flowing through your body's power centers. If you feel discomfort, go through this feeling into the magic that is available to you. During your moon cycle, your body is the sacred vehicle of the powers of the All That Is. You may take this opportunity to go through the doors to the other medicine powers that will put you on the pathway to experiencing the Web of Life."

When Grandmother had finished speaking, the four elders held hands around the young woman and sang an honoring song. When the song ended, they returned to the cave door. There, the same three young girls who had accompanied Calf to the cave rejoined them. The girls each embraced Calf and presented her with flowers. Spider Woman then burned the grasses used in the ceremony to return the gift of the moonlodge blood to its source.

The elders, Calf, and the young girls walked back to the village, where the whole tribe was gathered to welcome the new woman into their community. The People took turns congratulating Calf and many people gave her gifts. White Bison Calf wore her new painted skirt with her beautiful new hat, and felt the power of being a priestess. Grandmother led her to the place of honor in the circle as the tribe sat down to an honoring feast.

Chapter 4

The Celebration
of the Longest Night

Soon after White Bison Calf's initiation ceremony, winter came to the mountain valley of
the People of the Painted Earth Temple.
Snow covered the round thatched tribal lodges,
which appeared to be small hills with openings in
the east to welcome the light of the morning sun.
The People built their homes by first placing poles
in a circle in the ground, then bending them into an
arc across the middle of the circle. They tied the
poles together at the top to form a dome-shaped
room. Then they wove smaller poles throughout
the arched poles like a basket. They tied bundles of
thatch to the encircling poles to keep out the wind
and rain, and in the wintertime they added more

thatch and woven mats to keep out the cold and hold in the warmth created inside.

The cooking was done outside the lodge when the weather allowed and many rocks were put into the fire. When the rocks reddened with the heat of the fire spirits, they were brought into the lodge and placed into a hole in the middle of the floor. These fire rocks kept the lodge warm and cozy. In stormy weather, a small hearth fire in the west of the room heated the lodge and the smoke found its way out through the thatched roof.

The People placed their round lodges in a large circle with a space left in the east. In the center of the lodge circle was a community lodge. It was similar to the smaller family lodges, but large enough to hold all the members of the tribe at the same time. The tribe used this community lodge for gatherings and celebrations of all kinds.

To the west of the central meeting lodge was the home of Spider Woman, where White Bison Calf spent most the winter. Grandmother taught Calf to weave baskets and told medicine stories. As they worked one cold morning, Spotted Cat joined them and they began to prepare for the Ceremony of the Longest Night. In this ceremony, the whole tribe celebrated the rebirth of the sun and each day becoming a little longer until midsummer. The three medicine friends made the offerings that would be given to the Sacred Solstice Tree. That evening, the whole tribe gathered in the nearby Sacred Grove around the Solstice Tree, which was in the center of their ceremonial circle.

Grandmother Spider Woman tied the first offering onto the tree. It was a small ivory carving of Mother Gaia. She then offered a prayer: "Earth Mother, we call you to the Solstice Tree at the time of Longest Night. We celebrate the gift of the sacred bodies you have given us so our spirits may walk on Gaia's Land. We thank you for your gifts that give us life. With the birth of a new cycle of seasons, we ask for peace and lasting abundance."

After the first offering, everyone took a turn at placing a gift on the tree along with a prayer that honored one of the medicine powers. The People had lovingly crafted offerings of such things as clay, leather, woven grass, seeds, dried fruit, and dried meat. There were tallow lamps shaped like different animals, plants, stars, the moon, the sun, elementals, goddesses, and gods. Soon the tree was covered with beautiful give-away offerings. As the sun set in the west over a marker rock, the small tallow lamps were lit in honor of the Creative Fire.

The Sacred Tree glowed and sparkled with all the offerings, and the tribal shaman, Tree Spirit, spoke. "The Solstice Tree is a way of seeing the All of Life. Her roots go deep into the earth to draw the life energies from our Mother Earth. The tree's arms reach out and up to the sky, reaching for the gift of radiant power from Father Sun."

The tribe sang songs that included all the powers, creatures, and beings that were given to the tree. Slowly, one by one, the lamps around the Solstice Tree burned out and it became completely dark. The singing ended when the last lamp flame flickered and died.

While the tribe sang the winter songs, Grandmother Spider Woman left the grove and went to the Painted Earth Temple. She entered the cave and proceeded to the room of the Creative Fire. On the altar burned a tallow lamp whose flame had been kept burning for many cycles of ages. The young priestesses kept adding more oil and new wicks as needed so that the ancient fire spirit would have food. The High Priestess lit a lamp from the Holy Fire and walked back to the ceremony. She arrived just as the singing stopped.

Spider Woman prayed over a pile of wood stacked higher than her head. "Sacred Sun, who is reborn this night, we celebrate the gift of life that you give to Gaia's Land." She then touched the flame of her lamp to the sticks and the Sacred Fire began to feast and dance upon the wood. The huge fire to the east of the Solstice Tree illuminated the darkness in the Sacred Grove. The People cheered and they danced around the Sacred Fire long into the night.

Every fire in all the lodges had been extinguished before the People came to the Longest Night ceremony. When they left the Sacred Grove, each family took a part of the flame from the Solstice Fire to rekindle the hearth in their homes.

The next morning, the animal powers celebrated the Sacred Tree with their own ceremony. Many birds and animals of all sizes gathered around the tree and feasted with relish on the tasty food offerings that had been gifted to the tree.

Chapter 5

The Initiation of Spotted Cat

Spotted Cat grew more excited, and a little anxious, as the time of his coming-of-age initiation drew close. This would be his first visit to the Painted Earth Temple that was held in great reverence throughout Gaia's Land. Visitors from tribes that still honored the Earth Goddess in the ancient way would sometimes travel here to do ceremony. Young boys traveled for many moon cycles to be able to have their initiation in this ancient and sacred cave temple.

As a small boy, Cat and two friends once found the entrance to a cave and decided to explore it. He borrowed an oil lamp from his lodge and met his friends at the cave. After kindling a fire and lighting the wick in the little bowl of tallow, the three young boys squeezed through the cave's small opening. Cat felt intense fear inside the cave and he had difficulty breathing. His mouth became very dry and his body glistened with sweat.

His friend, Singing Cricket, joked, "You smell like you are afraid, Cat."

Cat replied, "A little. I was just wondering how we will find our way back to the entrance when we cannot leave footprints on the rock."

Silence fell over the young boys as they too thought of the risk of getting lost. The long shapes that the rocks made from the ceiling to the floor started to look like animals and people from the spirit world. The shadows seemed to press in tighter and tighter against them.

Cricket spoke up. "We can take this soft white stone I found and leave marks on the walls of the cave like the twigs we break to leave a trail through the forest." They all breathed easier, and agreed that this was a good idea.

The boys continued deeper into the cave, and as they did, Spotted Cat's fear subsided. He began to enjoy the adventure. All at once the cave filled with dark, frenzied winged creatures. It was so sudden that Cat dropped the oil lamp and the three boys stood in blackness. Cat could feel the movement of the air created by the creatures in the still cave as they flew near his body. The black of the cave exceeded the blackest night and reminded him of Grandfather's stories of the Sacred Void, the blackness before creation.

"Bats!" cried Little Fox. "I hate bats! Why did you drop the lamp now?" Singing Cricket yelled in a shaky voice, "How will we find our way back through this blackness?"

Cat laughed at his two friends, "Now you two smell of fear."

Fox replied, "My uncle Bear taught me to make fire with my eyes covered so I could have light on a starless night." Soon a small glow emanated from the tinder that Fox carried with his firestones. There was very little oil left in the lamp bowl so, to Cat's relief, the three decided to return to the door of the cave. After that, whenever his friends mentioned returning to the cave he always found an excuse for not going.

Spotted Cat did not like to admit to having such a deep fear but he was very apprehensive about entering a cave again. He decided to talk to Tree Spirit, the tribal shaman, about his upcoming ceremony of initiation.

Cat spent most of the late winter day looking in the part of the forest where he had often seen Tree Spirit walking. He found Tree sitting in silence, looking into a canyon. Not wanting to disturb him,

Cat sat down to wait for the old shaman to finish his meditation.

The young boy tried to be still and silent like the shaman as Tree Spirit continued to sit, so motionless that Cat could not see him breathing. Cat felt as silent as the rock he sat upon, and his breath gradually slowed. After a while, a squirrel came bounding by and hopped right on Cat's leg, then continued running along. This puzzled Cat, for the squirrel seemed to treat him like he too was a rock.

More time passed and a flock of small birds came into the trees surrounding where Cat crouched. Then one of them landed on his shoulder like he was part of a tree. Cat soon realized that, without saying a word, the shaman had taught him an important lesson about stillness.

Sunset came and Tree Spirit turned to leave. He saw Spotted Cat sitting on the rock. "Well, Cat, how long have you been there?"

"About four hands movement of the sun through the sky," replied Cat. The old shaman seemed pleased at Cat's answer and asked if he had a question.

"Grandfather, once my friends and I explored a cave we had found and I experienced a horrible fear inside the confining blackness. How can I control this fear at the time of my initiation?"

Tree Spirit sat silent next to Spotted Cat for a while, then said:

"The ceremony of initiation is very complex and was created by our ancestors to help a young boy through a difficult life passage. When a young boy becomes an independent man, a type of death occurs. The death of youth gives birth to a new adult in the tribe. I can not say too much about the ceremony, for it may take away some of the medicine power you will receive. I would not even say this much to the other boys the way I have to you. This is because you have been chosen by Grandmother Spider Woman to be her apprentice. Since she has chosen you, it means you will become a shaman and one day conduct this ceremony yourself.

It is sometimes possible that a boy will die during initiation ceremonies, but the disruption caused to a tribe by a lack of initiation ceremonies may cause the death of many tribal members. Know that Grandmother has honored you in choosing you to receive the more mysterious lessons in life. Go into your coming-of-age ceremony like a hunter going against a dangerous animal. The hunter knows that death is a possibility in the hunt but he also knows that the life of the whole tribe depends upon his bravery.

The hunter must face death bravely so that the tribe may live."

Soon after his conversation with Tree Spirit, Spotted Cat lay sleeping in his lodge and had disturbing dreams. He awoke and wondered if he was still in the dreamtime, for he heard sounds and saw moonlight reflected on shapes moving through the lodge. A fire was kindled from the hearth embers and Cat saw two men coming toward him. Their bodies were painted to look like strange beasts and they grabbed him forcefully. Cat's mother screamed, "Please don't take my son."

The men yelled, "You will never see your son again!"

Cat was filled with fear as the men pulled him into the dark night. After a forced walk through the forest, Cat could see a clearing by the full moon light that he recognized to be next to the opening of the Painted Earth Temple. The man holding Spotted Cat said, "You must enter the cave alone and naked without a light. If you make it through the cave you will come out the other end of the mountain a man. If you try to come back out this opening, you will be killed."

He lifted his spear. "Spotted Cat, begin your journey!"

His heart pounding like a drum, Spotted Cat entered the crack in the mountain and started to feel his way down the inclined passage. He bumped his head on a low rock and saw stars moving around, although they cast no light in the black cave. He realized that the roof was getting lower and soon he had to crawl. The passage narrowed even further and he had to slither on his stomach like a snake. Fear of the blackness closed in around Cat and nearly paralyzed him. His breaths were short and shallow. He kept hearing Tree Spirit's voice in his head saying, "Be brave like a hunter facing death, so that the tribe may live." This voice pushed him on despite his fear. After a long distance of squeezing through the narrowing passage, he emerged into what seemed to be a large chamber.

Not sure how he should proceed, Cat stepped forward cautiously. He waved his arms to feel for a low ceiling and tested each step with his toe in case there might be a pit to fall into. Suddenly, a bright light illuminated the cave and blinded Cat for a moment. After his eyes adjusted to the light, he could see a herd of horses running by him. Above his head hovered the largest bull he had ever seen.

Looking around in the chamber, Cat saw four creatures that were half human and half animal sitting next to oil lamps. The creatures started to make animal sounds that eventually turned into a rhythmic chant and soon he could make out the words: "Out of death comes new life." Another creature with the body of a human and the head of a bird walked out of the shadows toward him. It painted Cat's body with spots and he realized that the paint made him look like his medicine animal, the snow leopard. This creature began to look more human and Cat could now see that what had appeared to be wings were really feathers attached to human arms. The bird's head was a skillfully crafted mask of painted wood and skins that looked like a heron. Likewise, the other creatures began to look more human. He could see that they wore the masks of an eagle, a lion, a bear, and a horse.

On the walls of the cave were the most wondrous paintings of animals he had ever seen. The horses were painted over bulges in the walls, so they were rounded as in real life and they seemed to be running. They were so realistic that Cat wondered if he had slipped into a dream world where rocks easily change into running horses. The heron man had the paw of a snow leopard in his hand and scraped it across Cat's chest, making four scratches that oozed blood down his body.

The heron man then grabbed Cat's arm and led him into the blackness of the cave again, but seemed to be able to see in the cave as he led Cat along at a normal walking pace. A cloud of bats flew by them but Cat's old fear did not grip him this time. He understood that bats could see in the cave without using their eyes. He closed his eyes and imagined how the bats were sensing their way through the dark cave. Using this bat medicine, he reached out and felt the walls of the cave to determine the shape of the tunnel in which they walked. Spotted Cat could now sense the size and shape of the cave. After a while, he recognized that the cave had circled around to join itself and that they had returned to the same place. After the heron man had led him by this same place four times, Cat felt that this walk had become a sacred journey.

They entered a small chamber about twice the height of a man. It was rounded and he heard the sound of a trickle of water in front of him. The heron man released his arm and Cat could sense the bird-man moving behind him and sitting on the floor. The small chamber suddenly became illuminated, and again the shock of the light pained Cat's eyes. When he focused his vision, he could see scores of different animals all around him. Again, he felt like he had slipped into the world of dreams. The many different animals, including a snow leopard, seemed to be alive even though they were painted on the walls of the small room. Water flowed out of a hole in the wall in front of him above an altar stone. A small pool at his feet collected the water, and made water music.

The heron man began to speak and Cat recognized the voice of Tree Spirit. "Spotted Cat, bless yourself with this holy water from our Mother." Cat washed his hands and face and patted his head with the water blessing. Tree Spirit continued:

"When we enter into this cave, we are returning into the body of Gaia the Earth Mother. This room is the most holy part of her sacred body. This place is the womb that gives birth to all of earth's creatures. When a human or animal dies, their body returns to Mother Earth's body and their spirit returns to the One Spirit. When a spirit chooses to return into a body, the substance of their body is given again from Gaia, from her own body.

Birthing is difficult and painful, like the small passages you crawled through, as are many of life's challenges. The pain in life is a small thing compared to its wondrous gifts. When you leave this Painted Earth Temple, you will be a man of the tribe. It will be your responsibility to help provide for and protect the people of our tribe. Remember that all women are a reflection of Gaia in human form and should be respected, just as we honor and respect the Mother Earth.

You should not talk about what happened to you in this ceremony. If young boys knew what to expect in their initiation, they would not receive the full medicine. The mystery, the fear, and the story that the ceremony tells us are celebrations of this life passage. If the full power were not experienced, then the passage that is being honored would be made more difficult for a young boy becoming a man."

The heron man thrust Cat into the darkness again. "Follow this passage until you come to another door. You will leave that door as a man." Spotted Cat followed the upward-sloping tunnel. In the blackness a star like speck of light grew in size and soon became the cave opening he sought.

Cat walked through the door into the blinding brightness of day and found himself surrounded by the men of the tribe. Standing Bear approached Cat and embraced him. "Spotted Cat, we welcome you as a man and ask you to hunt for the People of the Painted Earth Temple." The men all placed hands on his body and sang an honoring song.

Chapter 6

The Celebration of East Star

The white blanket of snow that covered the Earth during her winter sleep started to turn into trickles of water in the springtime sun. These small water spirits crept down into the larger streams below. The streams then wound singing to join the River Goddess who flowed into the Great Water Goddess surrounding Gaia's Land. The small yellow elementals that were always the first flowers of spring started dancing between the few remaining patches of snow. The excitement in the village centered on the next important ceremony, the Spring Equinox. The People celebrated this equal day and night time as East Star, the Morning Star of the virgin birth.

As the time of East Star drew near, Grandmother Spider Woman, White Bison Calf, and Spotted Cat went hunting for eggs for the ceremony. Calf and Spider Woman hunted mostly for the nests of the give-away ground birds. These birds that provided so much food for the tribe also had nests that contained many eggs. When they found a nest, they took three eggs, leaving the rest to become baby give-away birds.

Spotted Cat searched the trees for the nests of the sky birds and, whenever he found one, he would take only one egg from it. Searching the trees could be dangerous, for the nests were sometimes built on very thin branches. Also, the larger birds would sometimes attack the egg hunters. Cat's friend Cricket had scars on his back where an eagle had clawed him as he took an egg from her large nest.

Spotted Cat wanted to get an egg from a dragon bird nest. He was a bit frightened of these large white water birds with their long serpent-like necks. As a small boy, Cat had once blundered into one of these nests and the large bird had chased him out of her territory. But this time he had a plan, and he talked Calf into helping him get a dragon egg.

Cat was hesitant because one of the dragon bird parents always remained near the nest. He had White Bison Calf creep close to the nest and, when the great bird attacked, streak away from the nest with the bird in pursuit. Spotted Cat ran up to the nest, and as he did he was amazed to see how fast Calf was running. This distraction caused him to trip on a branch and he fell headfirst into the nest, smashing an egg all over his face. Dazed, he picked up one of the remaining large eggs. Unluckily, the bird's mate heard the commotion and the father dragon bird was on Cat in an instant, attacking like an enraged demon. The angry bird whacked Cat in the head with his large wings and pinched Cat's back with his beak. Although sore and bruised, Cat managed to escape. Later, he proudly gave Grandmother the huge egg he had snatched from the dragon bird's nest.

The most enjoyable part of preparing for the ceremony was when the three medicine friends decorated the eggs to use as an offering to East Star. White Bison Calf took the dragon egg in her hand and painted Mother Gaia surrounded by flowers. They decorated the smaller eggs with pictures of gods, goddesses, animal powers, and many different flowers.

Cat asked Grandmother why painted eggs were given as an offering to the Morning Star. Spider Woman closed her eyes for a moment before she spoke:

"Spring is the time of the creation of new life. The East Star has phases of brightness much like the moon and she is also the brightest star in the sky. As the Morning Star shining in the east just before the sunrise, she is like the Virgin Goddess awaking a new day with life.

Later, the Morning Star joins with the sun for a while and is not seen in the sky. During this time, she is the Mother Goddess nurturing life. Then she parts from the sun as the Evening Star or the West Star. As the West Star, she is the first star we see at night and follows the sun soon after he sets. When she is the Evening Star, she is touched by time and becomes the Crone Mother Goddess. The Crone is the Wise Woman, keeper of the stories and ceremonies.

Eggs are a symbol of potential new life like the season of spring. The East Star is the Spring Goddess, and the time of equal day and night is her holy day. That is why we place painted eggs and flowers on her altar. This year, the Wise Woman Council has chosen you, Calf, to be the Priestess of the East Star, and you will sit with me at the altar."

Hearing this made White Bison Calf's eyes sparkle with excitement.

The ceremony began with a parade through the village. The children of the tribe wore their most brightly painted clothes and carried baskets of decorated eggs and flowers. While parading, they danced, sang, and played beautifully carved flutes. At the beginning of the line of dancers, four men carried two poles on their shoulders; on them was tied a seat. White Bison Calf sat in the chair as the Priestess of the East Star. She wore no clothes, although her body was decorated with garlands of flowers around her head, neck, waist, wrists, and ankles. She truly looked like the Goddess of Spring in her radiant decorations.

When the parade reached the floral altar in front of the Sacred Tree, Calf joined Grandmother Spider Woman sitting behind the flowers. Like White Bison Calf, Grandmother wore only the flowers of spring. All the children placed baskets of painted eggs and flowers at the altar and continued dancing around the priestesses.

After a while, the children sat on the ground while Grandmother told them a story about the Goddess of Spring.

"Long ago, there was a very bad winter and all the people and animals suffered from the cold. A little girl was out gathering firewood for her family and she found a small bird frozen to the ground. It seemed to be dead, and the girl prayed to the East Star to come and save the bird. The Goddess of the East Star heard the prayer and rode to Earth on a rainbow. Wherever she touched the ground with her feet, the snow melted and spring flowers emerged. The bird had frozen to death so the Goddess picked it up and blew her breath upon it. The bird came to life once again and it changed into a hare.

By now the goddess had brought spring to the Earth and flowers bloomed everywhere. The bird-hare was so happy to be warm that she started laying eggs. The eggs were all the colors of the rainbow and that is why we decorate eggs in honor of the East Star in spring."

During the telling of this story, the older villagers took the baskets and hid the painted eggs all around the village. After the High Priestess had finished, the children ran through the village hunting for the East Star eggs. The children loved this part of the ceremony and their laughter and squeals echoed like beautiful music through the village. When the children had filled their baskets, they took them to the Earth Father's pole.

This large pole was the height of four men, with a set of deer antlers attached to the top. It was erected within the Sacred Grove in the middle of East Star's flower altar. Many ropes painted the colors of the rainbow had been tied near the horns on the pole. The children each grabbed a rope, alternating a girl then a boy all around the pole. A song to the Horned Shaman started with everyone clapping.

The children danced around the pole. After a while, the music changed and the villagers started singing the Goddess East Star's song. The dancers had all been dancing sunwise around the pole. Now, the boys switched and danced in the opposite direction in a circle outside the girls. After the villagers finished the East Star's song, they sang a song to the Sacred Twins of Creation. The girls wove in and out among the circling boys, causing the ropes to weave a basket around the top of the Horned Earth Father's pole. As the dance ended, the sacred basket symbol of Earth Mother beautifully surrounded the sacred symbol of Earth Father.

With the whole village circled around the entwined symbols of the Earth Goddess and Earth God, they sat down to eat. To begin the feast, each person chose one of the colorful eggs and made a prayer to the power that was painted in its design, before eating the East Star offering.

The villagers' feasting continued until the sun crept below the horizon. Then they kindled a large fire and the whole village played music and danced in ecstasy. After a while, couples began leaving the dance to find a quiet place to lie down together under the moon and stars. In the final part of the ceremony, the couples gave sacred love medicine to each other and to the Goddess of the East Star. The pairs, for a while, embodied the splendor of Earth Mother and Earth Father in their rapture of creation. In this way, they gave a prayer to the Earth for an abundant spring.

Calf watched Spotted Cat as he danced glistening in the firelight. Having at last started her moon cycle and completing her initiation in the Painted Earth Temple, White Bison Calf was now permitted to join in this part of the East Star ceremony. She went to Spotted Cat and gently took him by the hand and led him into the forest.

He too had been thinking about this part of the spring ceremony. Grandmother had told him that during this union, a couple became united briefly with the Sacred Twins of Creation. He was happy that Calf had chosen him but also a bit nervous at the same time.

Calf took him to her favorite place, covered with flowers and next to a small cascading stream. The singing water blended with the fading music of the dance. Spotted Cat was her best friend and constant companion, and so she felt no hesitation, only a deep love and excitement as she pulled him down with her onto the flowers that glowed faintly in the full moon's gentle light.

The Celebration
of the Longest Day

O ne day, Spotted Cat and White Bison
Calf talked about their medicine animal
helpers. They decided to ask Tree Spirit
about how the People came to have such a close
relationship with the animal powers.

Tree Spirit sat outside his lodge, painting a
healing ceremonial shirt for Vision Wolf. Calf and
Cat approached him and quietly sat close by to
watch as Tree Spirit brought a wolf into a radiant
lifelike presence on the shirt.

As the old shaman painted, Calf asked, "Why
do we celebrate our animal powers with our names
and with paintings like the shirt you are making
for Wolf?"

Tree Spirit looked up from his work and smiled as he answered:

"The First Man who walked on Mother Earth watched very closely how the animals lived on Gaia. He understood that all the animal powers had a gift that he could use in healing or in teaching balance.

The children did not share the memories of creation like First Woman and Man. The children seemed to have forgotten that Mother Sky and Father Sky had created all life. Also, they forgot that every creature was part of the same family within the Sacred Balance. First Man called a council of several power animals to help him find a path of balance for the children to follow. The animals joining the circle were Turtle Mother, Whale Father, Fox Mother, Eagle Mother, Snake Father, Deer Mother, and Bison Father.

First Man explained why he had called a council meeting, 'I invite you to share with me the medicine power that creation has gifted to you. I need you to speak your wisdom to me so that I may teach the human children the Sacred Balance of Mother Earth.'

Turtle Mother spoke first in the council circle. 'The turtle tribe has a strong connection to the wisdom of the Earth Mother. We can hear the heartbeat of Gaia's Land, and that sound helps us to stay connected to our heart center. Horned Shaman, if you take a turtle shell and stretch a skin across it you will have a drum. Take this drum and make a heart-beat sound with a stick for your children. When they hear this drum sound, it will open their hearts, connecting them to Mother Earth and to each other.'

Whale Father spoke next. 'In the whale tribe, we sing songs to help us remember the stories of our ancestors. If you have a story that teaches balance, put it into a song to be sung along with Turtle's drum. This will help your children remember the wisdom of their ancestors.'

Fox Mother was next to offer her gift of words to the council. 'If you watch the fox tribe, you will learn of trickery. We often use tricks to catch small animals when hunting them for food. First Man, if you teach your children with words to help them learn about balance, the teaching may only be understood in their minds. Try to find a way to trick them into discovering for themselves the answer to a problem, and both their hearts and minds will understand the answer. The teaching will then be an experience that becomes a deeper part of your children.'

Eagle Mother took her turn at speaking. 'Creation has gifted me with the greatest vision of all the animals. I see everything from horizon to horizon when I look down from the sky. Most human children seem to focus on only one object at a time and they have a very limited view. Horned Shaman, you should teach the children to expand their vision to include the things surrounding what is in front of their eyes. In this way, when they face a problem, the children will understand that it is but a small piece of a larger reality, which includes its answer. Also, with this wider vision they will see how everything is connected.'"

A shrill call whistled above them and they looked up to see an eagle soaring. Tree Spirit lifted his arms, pointing his hands toward the medicine gift to acknowledge the eagle's blessing. He then touched his heart before continuing the story:

"Snake Father then offered his power to the council. 'Most people believe that I am lazy and sleep most of the time. Yet I am very much aware of the world around me. As I lie on the limb of a tree, I journey inward to the center of my being, collecting all my powers into my heart circle. From this place, I become aware of all my surroundings and I become one with all life. In this place of oneness, I receive the wisdom of my medicine power. First Man, if you teach your children to go to their centers of being, they will find peace within their place in creation. Also, have your children study the way I coil and climb in a spiral. They will see reflected in my movements how the energy of creation travels within their own bodies.'

Deer Mother next gave her wisdom to the council. 'Teach your children to respect the circle of life and death. Your tribe will always hunt the deer tribe for food. As long as the life it takes from my tribe is honored, the earth dance will reflect balance. The hunter will die one day and his body will feed the grasses. The grasses will feed the deer and the circle of give-away will be complete. If you teach your children this ceremony, they will know that the spirit never dies. Also, they will see that the bodies that were gifted to us by Mother Earth will always be food for new life.'

Bison Father's voice rumbled through the council. 'When my tribe is attacked, we form a circle around our young to protect them. In this way, Bison are the keepers of the Sacred Circle. The sun and the moon and the seasons are in a circle, as is the horizon of our world. Like the birds, you build round homes. First Man, your children tend to see life as a line from past to future. In truth, life is a circle and we are in its center within the eternal present. Teach your children that the circle represents life and it will help them to find the Sacred Balance.'"

The sun blazed overhead and Tree Spirit wiped the sweat from his forehead. He put the finishing touches on his painting before he concluded the story.

"The First Man now saw what a wonderful gift the animal powers had given him in this council. As the Horned Shaman, he was to become the teacher of these gifts. It would be his responsibility to pass this medicine from the animals to the future generations of people. And in the future, it will remain the role of the shamans to teach the wisdom of the animal powers."

The two young medicine friends left Tree Spirit and strolled through the village. It seemed like everyone was talking about the Solstice Ceremony. The summer pointer stone in the Sacred Grove cast a shadow from the rising sun that grew ever closer to the center Sacred Tree.

Grandmother Spider Woman started preparations for the ceremonies that would celebrate the Longest Day. About half of the people in the village had pledged to dance to the tree in the center of the grove. During the four days of the dance, the pledgers would fast, going without food or water.

The Sacred Tree symbolized Mother Earth. The entire family of plants and trees shared the prayers given to it. Every day during the whole change of seasons, the young priestesses wore long, beautifully painted leather skirts and gave offerings of food to the tree. On the Holy Longest Day, all the people who danced in the ceremony wore leather skirts like the priestesses.

The ceremony began before dawn and all the dancers sat between the Sacred Tree and the pointer stone facing east. As the sun rose over the marker, they gifted four songs to the sunrise honoring the four elemental powers that provide physical life. Spider Woman led the songs to earth and water, and Tree Spirit led the songs to fire and air. Next, Tree Spirit and Spider Woman went to the west end of the Sacred Grove and the other dancers formed a circle within this grove and around the Sacred Tree. To the east, there was an opening in the circle of trees to leave a door for the morning sun to enter and bless the ceremonial tree. The women dancers formed the northern half of the circle and the men formed the other half in the south. The singers and drummers sat on either side of the sun's doorway. They took turns singing and drumming, and the drumbeat and songs continued for the entire four days and three nights of the ceremony. At night, the villagers kindled a fire in this east doorway to illuminate the Sacred Grove.

With each dance, a pledger would take a prayer to the Sacred Tree for healing, thankfulness, or abundance. Also, they pledged to their community the special individual gifts within each human that may be given to the tribe. The pledgers could either dance or sit to meditate, as they felt inspired to do. Also, they could sleep and dream at any time during the dance.

The pledgers danced together in toward the center of their circle with the drums and song, and then danced backward, always keeping their eyes on the Sacred Tree. The wave of dancers going in and out became like a gradual and rhythmic inhaling and exhaling of breath. Soon it felt as if the Sacred Grove itself breathed in this rhythm. With each dancing breath, the Sacred Tree would receive the pledgers' prayers and give them to Mother Earth.

On the morning of the fourth day of the ceremony, the families of the dancers brought baskets filled with fruit, herbs, seeds, meat, and flowers. The dancers placed these offerings around the foot of the tree, arranged in beautiful decorations, and offered a prayer with each one. The Sacred Tree thus became a representation of the source of life's abundance.

White Bison Calf and two other priestesses left the Sacred Grove and went to the Painted Earth Temple. They carried water baskets filled with flowers. The priestesses walked through the cave to the womb chamber of the Temple. As the three young women sat around the Sacred Spring, they sang an honoring song. They offered the flowers to the spring as well. The three then returned to the Sacred Grove after filling the baskets with water spirits.

The dancers continued dancing to the beat of the drums until midday. When the sun was directly above the tree, the singing and dancing stopped and the priestesses entered the grove with their water baskets. Grandmother Spider Woman prayed over the baskets. "Sacred Water from the womb of Mother Earth, we give thanks for all your powers, the clouds, and their children the rains, the winter dance of snow and ice, the singing streams, river goddesses, and the Great Water Mother that surrounds Gaia's Land. In these medicine powers you bring life to Mother Earth and all her children."

The priestesses gave the water they had gathered to the Longest Day dancers. As the water passed from dancer to dancer, each one offered a small amount to Mother Earth and then drank for the first time in four days. When the dancers drank, they had a heightened understanding of what a precious gift to life the water spirits bring.

After the sacred water was passed around the circle, Grandfather Tree Spirit blessed the food. "To all the plants and animals that gave your life for this feast, we thank you. We honor the give-away that the Circle of Life has given to us. May we take this gift into our bodies so that our lives may be a special gift to all."

The whole tribe feasted on the food that had been blessed by the Sacred Tree and the Longest Day ceremony. The feasting and games lasted until nightfall. The People of the Painted Earth Temple knew that now, with each sunset, the days would become shorter as the sun journeyed south along the horizon again.

The Celebration
of the Harvest Moon

Running Horse roused Spotted Cat early one morning. "Cat, it is time to start your training as a hunter." The two men walked into the forest carrying their spears. Ever since he was a small boy, Cat had played at spear throwing with his friends. He had a natural ability and often won the games the boys created to test their skills. Running Horse had many skills to teach Cat that would perfect and enhance this natural ability.

Sitting with Cat in the forest later, Horse told him:

"You must find the way of hunting that is best for you. We learn by watching the different hunting animals and how they approach their kill. Some animals, like the snake, teach ambush hunting. A small creature will not feel any danger from a snake when it becomes so still that it looks much like the limb of a tree it lies upon. When the prey is close enough, the snake moves quicker than a blink of the eye. A hunter aligned with this way will paint his body to look like the forest, and then hide beside a trail that shows the sign of animals that have passed by. If the hidden hunter can get downwind from the prey, he can throw his spear before the animal is aware of his presence.

Animals like your medicine animal, the leopard, stalk their prey. They creep very quietly to follow the trail of, let us say, a deer. If the deer looks up and sees the stalking leopard or hunter, the stalker must freeze. If the deer continues eating, the stalker then knows he has been accepted as part of the forest, no different from a tree. The hunter may have to remain still for a long time. When the deer again lowers its head to eat, the hunter creeps closer until he is close enough to throw a spear.

Also, there are the pack hunters. To learn this way, watch how the wolves hunt.

They will look at the herd to see which animal is the weakest. One of the pack will then run at the animal and chase it until the wolf tires, and then another wolf will take over the chase. When the prey is winded, the whole pack moves in for the kill. Most of the hunters of our tribe like to hunt in this fashion. You must choose your best way for yourself. So I am sending you into the forest to live with the animals for one moon. Watch, and learn, and see which way of hunting speaks to you."

Spotted Cat still had not killed a large herd animal after many days alone in the forest, but he had speared fish and killed a few give-away birds with his slingshot for food. He walked along quietly and came upon a great owl a few steps away in a nearby tree. The owl looked into his eyes, then slowly turned its head to look around the forest. Spotted Cat could see that the owl did not focus on individual objects the way Cat did. Even when the owl appeared to look directly into Cat's eyes, its vision seemed to encompass everything in the surrounding forest. Spotted Cat used his newly learned owl vision to hunt for the rest of the day.

Using his new skill, Cat saw many more animals than he had ever seen before. Also, he found that when he did not focus directly on the animals he encountered, they would not run away. They seemed to feel that they were safely hidden from him because of their body markings and coloring. At times, just for fun, Cat would stop next to one of these "hidden" animals, turn in its direction, and stare at it. He could feel the tension rise in the animal as he touched it with his eyes. A thrill shot through Cat's body when this stalking was successful. He soon understood why Horse had sent him into the forest to learn from its creatures. He also realized that the stalking method of hunting used by his medicine animal was his method of choice as well.

The next day, Spotted Cat painted his body to look like the trees. As he walked through tall grass, two deer raised their heads from where they were bedded down. Cat froze with one foot in the air. His leg started to feel shaky after a while and the deer still watched him. Very slowly, and over a period of many breaths, Cat lowered his foot. The deer did not react to his motion. Using the same deliberate movement, he walked on, never looking at them, until a tree stood between him and the deer.

Using the tree's cover, Cat was now able to creep very close to the two deer. When he got close enough to throw a spear, he stepped out from behind the tree. Both deer snapped their heads up to look at him. Cat's spear hand was not ready, so he froze again. One of the deer walked toward him, sniffing the air. Cat was glad that the wind blew in his face, carrying his scent away from her. The deer then stomped her foot at Cat, who stood as still as a tree. Soon, she seemed to forget what had distracted her and lowered her head to continue grazing. At this distance, Cat could not miss and his spear struck deeply into the deer's heart. She fell dead onto the ground and her companion bolted away into the forest.

Cat honored the deer with a give-away song taught to him by Running Horse. He laid a hand on the deer and prayed to her spirit. After removing the internal body powers of the deer, he placed her heart in a tree for the eagles. Running Horse told him that these great birds would take the spirit of the deer and connect it to the powers of the Sky and Earth. He then took the liver and wrapped it in leaves as an offering to the Gaia Priestess.

In the ancient traditional way, Cat had become a hunter. As he headed for the village, he felt very different from the young man who had entered the forest alone many days ago. He realized that this, his first kill of an animal that would feed many people, marked the last part of his ceremony of initiation. It was especially meaningful because this deer would be a part of the feasting in the Harvest

Moon ceremony. As Cat entered the village, some of the villagers patted him on the back to acknowledge his becoming one of the People's hunters.

There was much excitement in the village when Cat returned because the Autumn Equinox approached, the second time during a cycle of seasons of equal day and night. Some of the People were away hunting for the animals that would give-away for the harvest feast. The children helped to pick berries and gather seeds. Many villagers picked fruit and dug roots for the great meal that would feed the People, their ancestors, and the animal spirits.

The next day, White Bison Calf and Spotted Cat helped Spider Woman hollow out turnip roots and carve faces on them. In the Harvest Moon ceremony, they placed oil lamps inside these roots so the faces glowed with eerie expressions. Also, they made masks with wood, leather, bark, and leaves. The masks represented their ancestors and the many different animal powers. Clothes worn with the masks represented the different spirits that the People honored in the ceremony.

"Grandmother," Spotted Cat asked, "Why do we make the carved turnip faces to look so scary? This has always been my favorite ceremony, but I do not understand many of the hidden messages in the things we do."

Spider Woman smiled and replied:

"At this time of the year, the leaves are dying, falling from the trees. In their death dance, Mother Gaia celebrates their passage by painting them in many beautiful colors. In this season when the door between life and death opens for a while, it is the time to honor our relations in the spirit world. The people and animals who have crossed over into the World of Spirit are still in a relationship with us.

That is why we leave offerings of food for them during our feast. To the animals that have given their lives to us that we may live we also present food offerings during the feast. In this way, they will know that we appreciate their give-away. Also, our ancestors will know that we appreciate all the gifts they have passed down to us.

Dancing while wearing masks is another way to celebrate the powers in the spirit world. As the villagers dance, spirits may join and share their power with the dancers. In that joining, the dancers experience the spirit world and learn many things from the other side.

The carved root faces are an offering to the spirits of people who have died and not accepted the beauty of the change of form that we call death. They cling to physical life, for they do not understand that to die is not the end. It is only a part of the cycle of rebirth. The glowing scary faces show that these clinging spirits are not welcome in our village. Our ancestors who have accepted the sacredness of both life and death can reach out to us in a helpful way. The others can be annoying and should be made to know that they must stay away."

The time of equal day and night finally arrived and Grandmother and her apprentices gathered the many-colored fall leaves. They also collected a huge pile of firewood for the ceremony. An altar stood in the east gate of the Sacred Grove. On the altar was a carved figure of Mother Gaia surrounded with the blazing colors of the autumn leaves. Abundant food from the fall harvest lay around the Goddess figure.

A large circle of skins had been placed around the altar where the villagers and spirits would sit during the feast. On the skins were twice as many woven grass trays for food as there were villagers. This was a way to invite as many spirits to the ceremony as there were people in the village.

Soon, the People of the Painted Earth Temple arrived. The food had taken a long time to prepare, and after fasting all day everyone was eager to eat. The feasting lasted all afternoon and the whole village felt satisfied and joyful.

When the spirits and villagers finished the great feast, Tree Spirit spoke to the Harvest Moon gathering.

"We are thankful to Gaia for the abundance of food and other blessings during this cycle of seasons. We are thankful for the ancestors and the animal powers who have joined us for this feast.

As each of you leaves the feast, pick up one of the fall leaves around Gaia's altar. While holding the leaf, think about something in your life that you would like to change. It may be a pain in your feeling awareness, or an illness, or a habit that you wish to have leave your life. Let the leaf become the unwanted thing. Then place it into the small fire in front of the altar and let the smoke carry it away. After this throw-away ceremony, go to your homes and change into the animal or ancestor of your choice and return for the evening part of the ceremony."

When the People returned, firewood had replaced the altar and a large fire burned. Surrounding the fire were the glowing faces of the carved turnip roots, looking out at the gathering. In the flickering fire-light, the villagers appeared to be transformed into spirit powers. Cat was dressed as his totem animal, the snow leopard. Calf wore a white bison mask and a white fur robe.

The drumming and singing began and the spirit powers danced around the fire. As Calf danced, she felt an immense power entering her body. This great strength caused her to imitate the movements of a bison. She stomped and pawed the ground as her animal power joined with her in the ceremony. She could feel the bison spirits' encircling protective power guarding the herd. She could sense the thoughts that the whole bison herd shared. This thought-sharing helped the herd to move with one mind.

As the night went on, the tribe's elders slipped out of the ceremony to return to their lodges, leaving the dancers and children behind. Soon after, the children returned to the village. On the way back to their homes, they pretended they were the displaced spirits who clung to life, as Spider Woman had explained to Cat. At most of the lodges there were carved turnip root faces glowing in the dark. Circling around the village lodges, the children would scratch on the woven mats that covered the lodge entrances. The village elders would peek out at the "ghosts" in their doorway. Gifts of honey seed cakes were given to these "spirits" so they would leave and not bother the lodges anymore.

At the Harvest Moon fire, shadowy spirits danced around the flames late into the night. By midnight, the fire spirits had eaten nearly all the wood. As the glowing embers died out, the dancers, like dreams dissolving, faded into the black night.

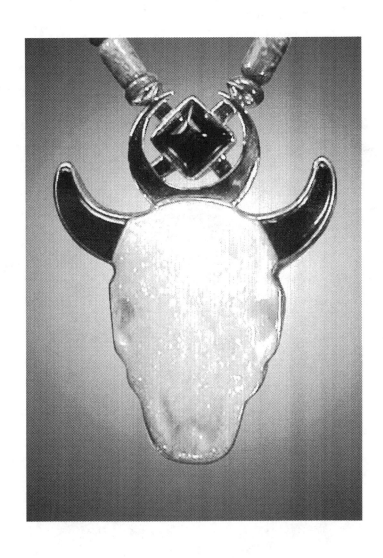

Chapter 9

The Fires of Change

Many winters passed and Spotted Cat had become respected as one of the best hunters in the tribe. One early spring day, several villagers went hunting. Cat wondered why the tribal shaman, Tree Spirit, accompanied the hunters, and as they walked along asked him, "Tree Spirit, are we going to do a special ceremony before we hunt today?"

The shaman replied, "The Slave Tribes, who worship the Thunder Storm God, have entered into the land where we sometimes hunt. We need to gather a council of our hunters to have a plan in case we encounter these dangerous people. This is a good place. Let us sit here in this clearing." The hunters gathered in a circle.

The tribal chief, Standing Bear, spoke first:

"The Slave Tribes began to kill and enslave the neighboring tribes who worship the Goddess after the severe winter when the sun did not shine over four seasons. I do not know why these tribes have chosen to make slaves out of people and animals. They keep large herds of captured animals so that they do not have to hunt for meat. Now our scouts have found tracks they made in our hunting forests and ride-on-the-backs-of-horses people accompany them.

We have heard bad stories from the surrounding tribes and we fear that if the Slave People see us, they may try to kill us. We have been taught to honor the Sacred Balance and to kill only for food, clothing, or shelter. It is not within the Sacred Balance to kill another human, but we must protect our families and ourselves. When a poisonous insect is in our lodge, it is within the Balance to kill it so our shelter will be safe. Our hunting grounds are an extension of our lodges, so it should be permitted to kill the Slave People to protect our home."

Tree Spirit looked grave as he answered:

"We must be careful that we do not become as unbalanced as the Slave Tribes. If we make what they call 'war' upon these tribes, we are like them. I feel we should fight back with our hunting tools only if we are attacked.

Also, we must find a way to study the Slave Tribes. Then we can learn, like we learn from watching a dangerous animal's habits, how best to avoid them.

For now, if they attack us while we are hunting, we should run to the thickest part of the forest. The ride-on-the-backs-of-horses people have the advantage in open spaces. Also, we are not skilled at fighting against other people with our axes. Our best defense would be to stay hidden and use our bows and arrows.

Grandmother Spider Woman feels that the whole tribe of the Painted Earth Temple will have to leave Gaia's Land and travel to Turtle Island. We will have a council of the whole tribe soon to talk about this. We need to be careful, yet we must also hunt to feed our families."

Star Raven, one of the tribe's few woman hunters, spoke. "I think it would be good to paint our bodies to look like the forest as we do when we become ambush hunters. If we encounter the Slave Tribes, we can then disappear easily into the forest. Also, we can agree upon various bird songs to communicate with each other if we find the Storm God People in our hunting grounds. Let us use the voice of the eagle if we see one of these people, the hawk's song if they see one of us, and three crow calls if we are attacked and need help from the other hunters." All of the hunters agreed with Raven's suggestions and they painted their bodies before leaving the clearing in search of animals.

Raven soon found the footprints of a large male deer. She followed the trail that led downhill toward a stream. The tracks joined the sign of other animals going to their place for drinking water.

Raven saw the buck drinking from the stream and quickly crouched down in the tall grass. Staying hidden in the grass, she crawled forward. She cocked her bow before rising on one knee to shoot. The deer looked up at her and Raven knew to aim a little forward of the heart. She expected the deer to jump forward, but he tried to jump up to avoid the arrow. The arrow struck the deer in such a place that it would take a while for him to die and he ran away.

Sitting still, Raven prayed to the deer's spirit not to run too far before lying down. Raven knew that if she didn't chase the deer, he would run a short distance, then lie down to rest and would be unable to rise. After a few moments, Raven followed the trail made by the deer. As the buck looked into Raven's eyes, she put a killing arrow into his neck.

Star Raven forgot about the Slave Tribe People as she sang a song to the give-away. As she started carving the deer with her flint knife, she heard a sound behind her. Turning around, she saw a large man swinging a strange-looking axe toward her head. She ducked and felt the axe brush against her hair. The Storm God Man had expected to crush Raven's head and was thrown off balance when he missed. Raven pushed him and he tumbled to the ground. She grabbed her bow and ran for the thickest brush. She crouched and hid and could hear the man walking toward her. When he got close enough, in one motion Raven jumped up and shot an arrow into his chest.

Raven gave three crow calls to summon the other hunters. Looking at the man she had killed, she felt sick to her stomach. She thought of all the honoring ceremonies that her medicine teachers had taught her, but was at a loss as to what kind of ceremony she should do now.

The tribal hunters arrived quickly and gathered around in silence. Everyone wanted to touch the man's war axe that was as hard as stone and as sharp as flint. It was very smooth, a beautiful color, and made a strange sound when struck by a rock. Standing Bear thought they should take the man's weapons back to the village.

Spotted Cat thought differently. "It does not feel like good medicine to have these strange weapons in our home. This is the first time that one from our tribe has killed another human. We must create a new ceremony for this Slave Man who tried to kill one of us. We should bury him with his weapons, and we should pray that his spirit may be reborn into a tribe where he can learn the Way of the Sacred Balance." The others, including Standing Bear, finally agreed that Cat was right, so they buried the man in the woods. They walked in stunned silence back to the village.

When the hunters returned with the deer that had given-away to Star Raven, a council was called in the community lodge. The villagers sat around the council fire that represented the future potential of the tribe. This potential was the children. All the decisions made in a council meeting were always measured against how they would affect the children's well-being, now and for the winters to come.

Grandmother Spider Woman spoke over the council fire.

"For many cycles of seasons, I have known that we would be overwhelmed by the changes that are occurring in Gaia's Land. Four Earth Ages ago, a new star appeared. It grew in size and came near to the Earth. When the star passed by, it caused devastating Earth changes. Land sank into the Great Water and mountains rose from the plains. The Sun's rays did not touch the earth for a long time. This was similar to the time when summer did not come to us, only much worse.

Before these upheavals, the seasons did not change and it was always like spring. The sun always rose in the east and set in the west the way it now does on the Spring Equinox and Autumn Equinox; all the days were equal in length.

Many tribes died during the harsh times after the changes. Some tribes abandoned the Sacred Balance Way and started forcing plants to grow and capturing animals to serve them. Other tribes made slaves out of other humans and the Sacred Balance became even more upset.

Our tribe is one of the few in Gaia's Land that still lives within the Sacred Balance as our ancestors did before the changes. The Painted Earth Temple is the last cave temple used in the ancient way.

In the new land of Turtle Island there are many tribes that practice the ancient teachings. The way of killing only for food, clothing, and shelter, as well as taking only from the Earth what she freely gives to us, is passing from our homeland. The way of never taking more from the Earth than we need, and always leaving some animals and seeds so they can reproduce themselves, also fades from our land.

If we stay, we would have to become warriors like the Slave Tribes. When making war, we would not have enough time to hunt and gather in the ancient, balanced way. In time we would become more and more like the Storm God People.

Those who wish to stay and join with relations in the other goddess tribes of Gaia's Land may do so. For the villagers who want to migrate to Turtle Island, we will start preparing to leave. The preparations may take a whole cycle of seasons.

I was planning for us to travel by way of the Great Water but that way is closed to us now, and we must look to the north. I suggest that Spotted Cat and Singing Cricket leave soon to find and check the trails. Far to the north are the Frozen Lands. Past the lands of forever winter are the lands of Turtle Island. When Cat and Cricket reach the Frozen Lands, Cricket will return with news of the safest trails for the People of the Painted Earth Temple. Spotted Cat will continue to Turtle Island and look for a place for us to build a new village in the New Land."

The next day, Spotted Cat and White Bison Calf spent the morning together visiting their favorite places in the Valley of the Nest. The two friends said their farewells at the stream where they had joined together at the East Star Ceremony several winters before.

Returning to the village, Cat and Calf joined the whole tribe for a safe-passage ceremony. Grandmother Spider Woman burned sage and blessed the travelers as she prayed: "Sacred Powers, we ask you to protect Singing Cricket and Spotted Cat as they journey north. May they find a safe trail that we can follow in their footsteps." The villagers sang a song while Cricket and Cat took up their traveling bundles and began their long journey. Just as they came to the edge of the nearby forest, Cat turned to look once more into the eyes of his dearest friend, Calf. Saddened, and apprehensive about leaving her and his tribe, he waved to her, then joined Cricket on the trail into the trees.

A cycle of seasons had gone by since Spotted Cat had left and, not for the first time, White Bison Calf was feeling sad. She missed him and feared for his life as he traveled through the hostile lands. She went to Grandmother Spider Woman and asked, "How did the Slave Tribes stray so far from the Sacred Balance?"

Grandmother spoke with sadness.

"After the great Earth changes, conditions were terrible for all of the tribes. The severe weather and land upheavals caused whole tribes of people and animals to die. Some creatures, like the insects, found the changes helpful and multiplied their numbers until huge clouds of them plagued the land.

Life was no longer joyful. It became a constant struggle for survival. Some tribes even started hunting and eating other humans. These tribes lost balance in their minds until they no longer resembled the humans who had once lived in the ancient Sacred Balance.

Even when conditions improved, some tribes held a strong fear of more horrible times yet to come. People feared that Earth changes might come again. The tribes started to grow large fields of grain with the seeds that at one time they had gathered from the wild. Other tribes captured animals and kept them in herds to use for food instead of hunting for meat as they needed it. They began to store more food than it was possible to eat in one cycle of seasons.

The slave animals and slave seeds that the tribes ate held less life energy. These changes, away from the way tribes had lived since creation, caused illnesses in the People. The stored food and overabundant meat caused all aspects of life to change. The tribes increased their numbers until the villages became very crowded. The abundance of nature could no longer support these large tribes now that they were no longer hunters and gatherers.

The way of our ancient ancestors, honoring everyone for their individual gifts, was no longer respected. The children in our tribe learn all the different activities necessary for the tribe's survival. Both girls and boys learn to hunt, to gather seeds, to weave, to cook, and to do ceremony. Most of the hunters in our tribe are men, yet if a woman finds that hunting is her greatest joy, she may join with the men. Also, if some of our men feel like weaving or cooking, they can do so.

The Slave People became very detached from each other and each person did only certain tasks. Only men were allowed to hunt, and then only if their father was a hunter. Only men could be shamans and lead ceremonies. Only the women could weave or take care of the children. These tribes became so far removed from the Sacred Balance that their minds and hearts were no longer able to embrace life in the way of their ancestors."

A great sadness enveloped White Bison Calf. Her heart seemed to be breaking as she saw how out of balance Gaia's Land had become, and she realized even more clearly the danger that surrounded her beloved Spotted Cat. Grandmother saw Calf's sadness and pulled Calf toward her in a loving embrace.

Soon after Calf's talk with Grandmother, Singing Cricket returned from his journey north. The People of the Painted Earth Temple planned a great feast to honor him.

Before the feast, there was a council meeting involving all the people of the tribe. The tribe focused its attention on a hide located in the middle of the council circle. On the hide, Spotted Cat and Cricket had painted pictures showing the mountains and grasslands they had walked through and the rivers they had seen. It showed villages that were helpful, friendly, and supportive. It also pointed out the dangerous areas to avoid. Cat and Cricket had drawn the places where they had seen the Slave Tribe People.

Cricket told wondrous stories about his long journey to the Frozen Lands. He described people who kept slave animals and plants but who also honored the Goddess and were welcoming to strangers. Also, every tribe he and Cat visited told stories of attacks by the warring Storm God People.

After the meeting, White Bison Calf pulled Cricket to one side and asked if Spotted Cat had sent a message to her. Cricket smiled. "Cat talked very much about how much he was missing you. At one of the villages where we stayed, the people had magical stones. The stones reminded Cat of a vision quest he had taken as a small boy. When the sun touched them, all the colors of the rainbow danced within them. Spotted Cat traded a basket woven by Spider Woman for one of these magical rocks. He then spent the evenings of many moon cycles carving the stone for a gift that I could bring to you."

Cricket handed Calf a small deerskin bundle. Inside was a white stone carved in the shape of a bison head. On the reverse side was a carving of the Goddess Gaia. It was tied to a thong so Calf could wear the carving as a necklace. In the sunlight, a glowing rainbow lived within the carved stone.

Soon the food was prepared and the whole village sat down to feast together. Singing Cricket kept telling stories and everyone directed their eyes toward him. As this went on, Spider Woman and Tree Spirit came to White Bison Calf and asked her to follow them.

The three medicine people slipped away and walked to the Painted Earth Temple. They went to the womb chamber of the Temple and sat in silence for a while before Grandmother spoke. "From hearing Cricket's stories, I think the trails to the north are more dangerous than I imagined. I do not feel the tribe has stored enough food for the journey, but I feel we should leave very soon. We will have to hunt and gather as we travel, which will cause us to go slower. Actually, the slower pace will be helpful for the elders and the children."

Grandmother, Tree, and Calf sat around the hide-drawn picture Cricket and Cat had made showing the trails to the north. They talked for a long time about the difficult choices of routes and what to carry on the great crossing to Turtle Island. None of them had traveled very far to the north.

Finally, they decided to tell the tribe to prepare to leave before the next crescent moon.

At the feast, Cricket felt like one of the heroes in the stories that Tree Spirit often told around the village fire. He thought of a good story and began to tell it. "When Cat and I were crossing the Great Grasslands, we came upon a camp of Slave People. The Storm God People were playing war games with sticks, fighting each other and using the sticks as spears and axes. We knew that if we were discovered, it would mean our death. So we crawled in the tall grass for the remainder of the day. Toward evening, Cat and I came to a wide river..." Singing Cricket gestured expansively with his hands to embellish his story. He spread his hands wide, and suddenly an arrow appeared sticking out of his forehead.

The villagers looked on in confused shock. Some of them even wondered for an instant if this was somehow just a trick, part of Cricket's story. As he slumped to the ground, a frightening cry surrounded the feasting villagers. Fear immobilized them momentarily, and then the air filled with arrows.

Some of the villagers ran for the forest and were met by several hairy men who killed them with axes. The men chopped the People of the Painted Earth Temple like firewood sticks as they shrieked their blood-curdling yells. Silence soon fell with the last of the defenseless villagers. The men pillaged the lodges, taking the meat and seeds that had been so carefully stored. Carrying the food in the People's beautifully woven baskets, they fled the now eerily still village.

Grandmother, Tree, and Calf left the cave. The thought of leaving the Painted Earth Temple forever made their hearts heavy as they walked back to the village. Twilight glowed in the east and they realized that their talk had lasted all night.

The three stopped short as they heard a faint moaning sound. Walking toward the sound, they found Blue Bird lying on the ground, blood pouring over one side of her face. She had a deep gash on her head and Grandmother began to treat the wound with herbs. Blue Bird sobbed, "A Slave Tribe attacked the feast and I think that everyone has been killed. They came at us without warning. There were many arrows in the air. The hunters did not have their hunting tools with which to fight back at the feast. After the rain of arrows, they rushed in with large axes to finish killing everyone ... even the young children. My children too ..." Bluebird slumped in anguished pain, and could say no more.

The four rushed to the village and stared in disbelief at all the blood and mutilated bodies strewn on the ground. White Bison Calf looked at the bloody remnants of her friends and community, feeling numb. Little Fox, who had survived the Storm God People's attack, came out of the forest. Shy Dove and Star Raven also joined the small group of villagers who were all that remained of the People of the Painted Earth Temple. All of the attack survivors had wounds and Calf found that helping to treat them had a calming effect on her.

Tree Spirit spoke sadly: "We must prepare a ceremony for our people. Too many of our family are dead for our normal burial ceremony, so we need to build a huge fire to send the villagers' bodies to the Earth and Sky."

Taking bundles of thatch and supporting poles from the village homes, they stacked a large pile of wood in the community lodge. Tearfully, they laid the lifeless bodies on top of what had once been their shelters.

The seven surviving villagers stood facing the entrance to the central lodge. They placed an ivory statue of Mother Gaia in the doorway. In front of this altar, they kindled a small fire. White Bison Calf took a bundle of sage and lit it with the fire. She purified herself and the others with its smoke and they all rubbed ashes on their bodies and in their hair.

Grandmother Spider Woman prayed: "I had dreamed of our community migrating to Turtle

Island where we could live in peace and within the Sacred Balance. Now nearly all of our tribe is in the World of Spirit. To all of our relatives, we look forward to a time when you may choose to be in a body again. Perhaps we will be together in a community of peace and love in the New Land." She reached down, took a burning branch from the altar, and threw it on the makeshift funeral pyre.

Blue Bird, still weeping, picked up a brand and spoke over it. "To my small children, Jumping Frog and Dragonfly, I grieve that we are separated. I send my love to you in the spirit world." She added this flame to the burning pyre and, still dazed, turned away.

Little Fox added his prayer to the roaring fire. "My anger wants to find the Slave Tribe that did this and kill them one at a time. I feel that if I were to follow my anger on this quest, the beauty that was our tribe would die in me. I pledge to continue to live and walk the teachings of Balance."

Star Raven next spoke to the fire. "I will travel west to the People of the White Horse. The three who are wounded may join me with my family there. We can heal our bodies in the village of my birth. Next to Mother River, we can build a new life and heal our grief."

Shy Dove added her voice to the flames. "To all my friends, family, and community, I hold in my heart all the beautiful times we have shared. All of the times of joy are like a sunrise in the darkness of last night."

White Bison Calf found it difficult to speak through her tears. "I will carry the beauty of the Sacred Balance and the Web of Life to the New Land. I will join with my mate, Spotted Cat, and I promise that we will birth a tribe dedicated to peace and balance."

Tree Spirit placed the last of the altar fire in the burning central lodge. "Sacred Fire, we appreciate your help in what should have been a burial ceremony. May the creative fire that Crow Father brought to us change our grief into acceptance of our life as it is on Mother Earth. We, who are the last People of the Painted Earth Temple, will always live the teachings of our ancestors that we love so well. With the ash, our tribal family returns to our Mother Earth. With the smoke, their spirits rise up to join with Sky Father and the One Spirit."

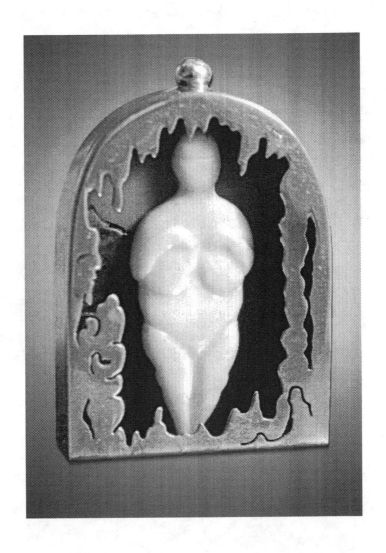

Chapter 10

The Sleeping Temple

Three days after the fire ceremony, Grandmother Spider Woman asked Calf to come to her lodge so they could discuss the upcoming journey to Turtle Island.

"White Bison Calf, you may have guessed that I will not be accompanying you on this journey. The Slave People now know about our village and they may attack again soon. The four of us who were wounded will join the White Horse People in the west. Life has chosen you for an important, yet difficult, adventure. In following your destiny, you will take the same trail as Spotted Cat.

I have tried to pass on to you as my apprentice the teachings of the Web of Life, and how all beings are connected. I have taught you the way of healing, the way of harmony, and the power of our ceremonies. Outside of Gaia's Land, the knowledge that you carry will blend and change with the New Land and the tribes of Turtle Island.

On Turtle Island you will find that there are many tribal peoples who have migrated across the Frozen Lands and over the Great Water. There, they continue a life of balance with the Mother Earth and the Web of Life. The New Lands are abundant with life, though very few people are there to share the abundance. The Slave Tribes have very little knowledge of Turtle Island. This is because the priests and priestesses of Gaia's Land have kept to themselves the secrets of guiding boats to the New Land and crossing the difficult trails of the Frozen Lands. It is impossible to cross the Great Water without knowledge of the guiding stars. Likewise it is impossible to cross the land of forever winter without the help of the tribes of the north. This will be your trail. The tribes in the north that still touch the earth in the way of the Sacred Balance will help you on your journey.

The People of the Sea experienced a great disaster and the water route to Turtle Island will be disrupted for many winters. This disaster caused us to experience the cycle of seasons that had no summer. It happened when the sacred mountain on the island of the Sea People broke apart and covered their island with burning rivers of rock, and covered the Earth with smoke. This was the year when the sun could not touch the earth and we had four seasons of winter.

The People of the Sea were free from attacks because the Slave Tribes did not have boats or the wisdom of the Sea People's star priestesses. Without guides or boats, the Slave People were dependent on the Island People for sea trade and could not make war on their islands.

The Sea People are a tribe that loves peace. They worship the Earth Goddess in cave temples as we do. After their island was destroyed, they began rebuilding a new village on another island. Much of their culture and their sea boats were lost, and they may never recover the full strength they once had.

I have known for a long time that our tribe needed to migrate to Turtle Island to escape the warring Slave Tribes. My plan was to travel by sea, but that is no longer possible. The four seasons of winter also caused much famine and the forced movement of many tribes. The Slave Tribe that attacked our village was probably pushed off their land by another warring tribe during these disruptions.

As you know, in the middle of the Frozen Lands, Spotted Cat continued to Turtle Island while Singing Cricket returned here. Since Cricket was killed in the attack, you will not have a guide. But you will have the painted skin that shows the trails north.

With most of our tribe gone, you will have to take this journey to Turtle Island with only Tree Spirit for company. I will stay here as the last Gaia Priestess of the Painted Earth Temple. I have given my life to the People, to the Sacred Balance of the Earth, and to the Web of Life. As my apprentices, you and Spotted Cat have learned the knowledge of Gaia's Land so that it may be reborn in the New Land. You two are now to be the keepers of the Way of Sacred Balance that has given our people happiness for many great ages of earth cycles. As you give-away the wisdom of Gaia's Land, it will help to bring peace and abundance to Turtle Island."

White Bison Calf sat gripped in the fear of having to journey for several winters. She asked, "How will I find Spotted Cat in the New Lands? To travel so far feels overwhelming."

Spider Woman sighed in understanding and said to Calf, "This is a huge task for a young priestess. Yet, remember that it is also a great honor to take this wonderful gift from Gaia to Turtle Island. You and Cat were born to share your lives, and your hearts will draw you together again. It is true that the New Lands are vast and it will not be easy to rejoin Spotted Cat. Before he left, I told him to find the heart of Turtle Island and give-away the teachings of the Web of Life. The teaching will spread out from this center to the surrounding tribes. When you find the Gaia teachings among the tribes, you will know that you are on the correct path to your sacred twin."

Calf worried aloud, "Grandmother, what is to become of you? When Tree and I leave on the journey you will be alone. Who will help you to hunt and gather food?"

Spider Woman smiled as she embraced Calf.

"My duties as High Priestess are now finished and it is your time to be the High Priestess. I know that you are young. Even so, the great responsibility you carry will help you to grow into your personal power. Your destiny is to build a new life in the New Land.

The old way has been overwhelmed in Gaia's Land, and for a while you can help the old way survive on Turtle Island. My place is to remain in the Painted Earth Temple, and your last task before you leave will be to close the door of the temple with me inside.

The temple that has helped our people for many ages of winters has finished her purpose. In my last ceremony as High Priestess I will put the temple to sleep, and I will then drink the herbs that will put me to sleep. The crossing to the New Lands is too difficult for me and I would only encumber your journey. Once I am in the spirit world I can easily travel there. I may be born into the body of your first child in a future time and we can be united again.

With that reunion, you will be my teacher in the ways of the Sacred Balance."

Tree Spirit prepared two bundles that the travelers would be wearing on their backs and in the morning the three remaining People of the Painted Earth Temple walked to the cave. Tree Spirit took Grandmother in his arms for a long hug and they both had radiant smiles as they parted. As White Bison Calf embraced her, Spider Woman gazed deep into Calf's tear-filled eyes and said, "After many winters we will be together again. Be strong and brave and you will be the Gaia Priestess bringing new life to Turtle Island."

With these words, Grandmother Spider Woman entered the cave. She walked to the womb chamber, blessed herself with water from the Sacred Spring, and laid out her medicine bundle. Taking out her painting tools, she drew a line from the white bison painted on one wall to the snow leopard on the opposite wall. The Priestess also drew a line from the spider over the door to the tree above the altar. She then drew lines between all the painted animals, forming a great spider web that connected all these creatures one to another in the Temple's most holy room.

Calf and Tree Spirit climbed the slopes above the small opening. There was a pile of large rocks that Tree Spirit had placed on a high ledge above the cave. He placed an offering of food and water next to the rocks. He then lit a bundle of sage. Calf and Tree Spirit blessed themselves with the sage smoke, and then he prayed, "Sacred Painted Earth Temple, we thank you for all you have given to our people. From the beginnings of our tribe, you have helped us in our ceremonies and initiations. It is with sadness that we must now say farewell to you and to Spider Woman. May she go shining on her way to the World of Spirit. It will be with joy that we welcome the time when we will join together with her again."

Tree Spirit removed a pole that supported the bottom rock and the stones tumbled down toward the temple door. This dislodged larger rocks to join in an avalanche of boulders that closed forever the door of the Painted Earth Temple.

Grandmother heard the rumble of the avalanche echoing through the Painted Earth Temple, and then a sudden silence. She took out the herbs she had brought and placed them in a bowl of water taken from the Sacred Spring, praying, "Sacred womb of the Earth Mother, you have been a wonderful sanctuary for the people. With the coming of the changes that surround us, I put you to sleep to protect you from being despoiled by the warring tribes. Be at peace knowing that through

116

you the Goddess has given her wisdom to many generations of children, and her gifts will continue to live on within their offspring. I rejoice to have lived as Spider Woman and the embodiment of the Goddess for our tribes. It has been an honor to be of service to my Mother Earth and my people. Sacred Goddess, watch over our grandchildren as they keep alive the wisdom of Gaia's Land in their new home." With a blissful smile, the High Priestess of Gaia drank the herbs and sang her medicine song until the oil lamp flickered and went out. As the light left the cave, she became one with Spirit, leaving her body sitting like the Gaia Goddess in the sleeping temple.

Chapter 11

The Journey of the Gaia Priestess

Tree Spirit and White Bison Calf looked down at the pile of boulders that covered the door of the Painted Earth Temple. Their hearts aching, they placed their bundles on their backs. Facing north, they took the first step of a journey that would see many cycles of seasons.

The first part of the trail took them through the familiar mountains surrounding their village. After two moons, the forest started to thin and the trees were not as tall as before. The mountains became smaller and more rounded. Some of the tribal people they visited on their journey had at one time traveled to the land of the People of the Painted Earth Temple.

White Bison Calf started to realize how well known Spider Woman was beyond their tribal boundaries. She also began to understand the huge responsibility she carried as the keeper of the knowledge of the last Gaia Priestess. The wisdom that had passed from Grandmother Spider Woman to her had gone from priestess to apprentice for many ages of winters. It would now be up to White Bison Calf to pass on the wisdom of the ancestors to the peoples of Turtle Island.

Many of the Slave Tribe People lived in the Great Grasslands below the North Forest and in the fertile river valleys. All the tribal people White Bison Calf and Tree Spirit visited told them stories about the Slave People pushing the Goddess tribes out of the more lush, productive lands and into the mountains. Contact with the Thunder God People usually ended in death, or capture and slavery to these fierce warriors.

Calf sat at a friendly village fire one night and talked to the tribal priestess about her journey north. As in most of the villages they had visited, she could not speak the language so she used hand signs to communicate. This common language always served when mixed groups of tribal people were together. When they used spoken words along with hand signs, each conversation became a lesson in which to learn another tribe's language.

As she asked about the trails, Calf realized that she and Tree Spirit could no longer avoid going through the Slave Tribe territories.

The priestess to whom she talked was named "The Daughter of Hela," the Mountain Fire Goddess of Creation. In the tribe's stories, the Earth Mother lived in a smoking mountain. The sacred cave of her village led to a room of fire that was the Goddess of Fire's womb. All life was born from this fiery womb and returned there to be reborn.

Hela told Calf, "When you arrive in the Forest Lands to the north of us, you will be safe. In the forest live the People of the Reindeer. The tribes of the North Forest honor the Goddess as the White Reindeer."

"I have heard stories of how the snow is very deep for much of the year," Calf replied. "In our village, travel becomes so difficult when the snow is deep that we live for several moon cycles on dried meat and gathered seeds without venturing far."

"The North People have adapted to the long times of winter," Hela said, then added:

"I have heard that they tie sticks to their feet so they can walk on top of the snow. They live in painted tents of skin and follow the migrations of large herds of reindeer. I am not sure that I believe all the stories that are told about the shamans of the north, but they are said to be powerful healers and singers.

It is said that the shamans can call reindeer with their drumming and songs. The deer will then allow the healers to tie rope from them to a slides-along-in-the-snow basket. These large baskets are similar to the drag poles that the Slave People sometimes tie to their horses so they can carry large bundles. The North People ride in the baskets pulled by the reindeer."

White Bison Calf anxiously asked, "Are the White Reindeer People a Slave Tribe?"

"I wondered myself about this when I heard these stories," Hela responded, and explained:

"The reindeer are from a wild herd and help the shamans as a give-away. They may then return to their wild herd and the Sacred Balance of Mother Earth. But the Storm God People use the animal tribes in a very different way. The Slave Tribes believe that the horses that serve them are inferior creatures that they can own. It is something they call 'property.' Also, this can mean one tribe can 'own' land, like all the land from a certain river to a certain mountain. If another tribal person walks across this 'property,' the Slave People may kill them or enslave them, even if they are from another Thunder God tribe.

The Slave Tribes also mutilate their male horses' genitalia so they cannot breed. Sometimes, an exceptionally large male horse will be the only one allowed to breed. This causes the whole herd to change its physical characteristics in a few generations. The effects that the Slave Tribes create in the Web of Life are changing the Sacred Balance forever. I feel that one day they will enslave all the goddess tribes in Gaia's Land. The animal tribes, the plant tribes, and the human tribes all are having a difficult time keeping the Sacred Gaia Balance in our homeland."

White Bison Calf thought of the land of her youth and the beautiful place that Hela's tribe lived in, and began to cry. Hela gathered Calf in her arms and the two priestesses wept together.

The next day, Tree Spirit led Calf to the top of the highest hill to view the surrounding land. From there, they could see the Grasslands stretching out to the horizon. Calf saw movement in the Sea of

Grass and dropped to the ground, pulling Tree after her. Many men on horses were riding through the flat land. They looked like warriors, for they carried large axes. The men led several horses with packs on their backs. Bound captives also rode a few horses, trailing the others.

Tree Spirit spoke quietly. "The warriors can see us from a great distance if we walk through this open land. Until we reach the North Forest, we must move only at night. We will have to eat our dried meat, berries, and seeds uncooked, for we cannot make a fire."

Night after night the two friends walked through the endless grass. During the day they would sleep in a depression in the ground or under the cover of sparse clumps of bushes. When they had walked for three cycles of the moon, mountains appeared in the distance. The ground became rolling hills and there were trees in the canyons. In a few days, they came to a large river flowing out of the mountains. There was vegetation along the banks and Tree Spirit thought it would be safe once more to walk during the day.

After walking for two more days, the travelers came to a place where the river had cut very high cliffs on both sides. The canyon walls were too steep to climb, and the two companions would have to stay in the deep canyon for a few days.

Toward sunset on the next day, Tree went hunting with his sling and Calf gathered wood for the first fire in three moons. But first she took a refreshing swim in the river. This brought on a feeling of well-being and she began to hum a song. Calf bent down to pick up a stick, and her body suddenly went numb as she was struck on the head by something from behind. She was barely conscious as her attacker bound her hands behind her back with a thong. He then hauled her up and pushed her to walk before him.

White Bison Calf had never seen a Slave Tribe person up close. His body was very hairy and his beard was matted. He smelled like he had never bathed in his whole life. Calf was amazed that he had crept close enough behind her to strike without her smelling him. He wore a bearskin tied at the waist with a large axe hanging from a thong. He also carried a bow and arrows in a bundle on his back.

If Calf walked too slowly, the man would jab her with the point of his spear. The trail on which they walked headed down the river from where Tree and Calf had just come. They came to a camp occupied by twenty or so warriors who looked, and smelled, the same as her captor.

Calf was pushed down beside two other women who were also bound. Both looked like they had been severely beaten. Guarding the women was a man seated next to them with an axe in his hand. The other men had killed a horse and were gathered around a fire to cook it, some distance away from their captives.

Calf heard a thud and the guard's head drooped forward. He looked like he had suddenly fallen asleep, but Calf quickly realized that he had been killed by a rock. Then Tree Spirit appeared at her side, winding up his sling. He cut the thongs and freed the three women as he whispered, "Calf, our packs are back there by that large tree on the hill. Take them and move upriver very quickly and leave no trail. I hoped to journey with you to the New Land but my fate is here. Like Spider Woman, my body is to stay in Gaia's Land, and today is a good day for my spirit to join Grandmother's." Calf's eyes filled with tears, yet she knew they had to move fast and there was only time for a loving embrace and a brief farewell glance into the eyes of Grandfather Tree Spirit.

Calf and the two women ran for the tree and picked up the traveling bundles and hunting tools. The men were so interested in the roasting horse that they had not noticed the captors' escape. Tree Spirit climbed a cliff near the camp to reach a high ledge. He shot his bow and one of the men at the fire dropped to the ground with an arrow in his neck.

The women ran up another hill, then stopped to catch their breath. Looking back, they saw that the Slave Tribe men could not hit Tree with their arrows because he could easily hide behind the ledge he was on. Walking back and forth on the ledge, he would peek over and drop one man at a time with an arrow. Soon, several men climbed up the cliff toward Tree, who had shot his last arrow. He then threw large rocks down on his enraged pursuers. He was able to fell some of the men with stones propelled from his deadly slingshot. Finally, Tree managed to push a huge rock off the ledge, which started an avalanche of boulders that knocked the remaining men off the cliff. Just as he pushed the rock off the ledge, an arrow found its mark and he tumbled forward into the rockslide he had started. Before Tree Spirit fell, he raised one hand toward Father Sun and placed his other hand on his heart to honor Mother Earth. With this gesture, the old shaman offered his last prayer.

Tears again welled up in White Bison Calf's eyes as the other two women frantically pulled her toward the upward-sloping trail. Her companions seemed to know where they were going, so Calf followed. Walking on rocky ground so as not to leave a trail, the three freed captives traveled all night. After a brief meal from the last of Calf's dried meat, they traveled all day. At nightfall, the women ate a meal of rabbit that had given-away to Calf's sling. The weary travelers napped briefly, then walked through the night again.

The next day, the three women came out of the canyon at a spot where the surrounding hills were covered with trees. While crossing a wide stream, they turned and walked upstream in the water. Eventually leaving the stream, they followed a trail that led to a small village where houses were made from skins stretched over poles. The poles were tied together at the top so the lodges were pointed to the sky. The round homes had a fire in the center and smoke found its way out where the poles were tied.

Calf and her new friends went to one of the painted lodges and sat down. Calf showed them the skin that Spotted Cat had painted, pointing to the river that the three of them had just followed. She showed them some pointed objects by an adjoining stream. Her traveling companions nodded in agreement that this represented their village.

Calf asked if the villagers had seen Spotted Cat, and one of them left to go into a tent. She soon returned holding a basket. White Bison Calf recognized Grandmother Spider Woman's design at once. Touching the carved rainbow bison hanging from her neck, she realized that this was where Cat had obtained the magical stone.

Chapter 12

The Wisdom of Drumming Deer

hite Bison Calf had found the Tribe of the the White Reindeer, and knew they were the people who had helped Spotted Cat on his journey. As she settled into the daily rhythms of the village, Calf felt her body healing from the fatigue of the many moon cycles she had spent walking to the North Forest. The villagers were friendly and she especially liked Drumming Deer. He was the tribal shaman, and the tribe held his powers in awe. His hair and beard were completely white and he often laughed. He wore brightly colored and decorated cloths like the rest of his tribe.

The villagers told stories of how Drumming Deer could shift his body shape into different animals. They said he would sometimes walk into another world and disappear for a moment. While in these other worlds, he could learn much about the animal powers. Also, he could bring back knowledge of healing herbs and ceremonies. The Reindeer People said that he had lived for almost an entire Earth Age. Calf had never heard of any human living such an amazing amount of time. That was ten times as long as Tree Spirit had lived, and her tribe considered him very old.

Since winter was on its way, Calf decided to live in this hospitable village until early spring. The journey through the Frozen Lands would be more difficult if she were to start out before then. Her new friends gave her beautiful clothes that were lined with fur. She particularly adored the fur-lined boots that were so much warmer than the ones worn by her tribe.

One day Calf visited Drumming Deer in his tent. The snow and wind howled outside, but even so it was warm and cozy next to the fire. He was sewing a pair of tribal boots beautifully decorated with intricate embroidery. The designs reminded Calf of the designs that Spider Woman liked to weave into her baskets. She watched his skillful hands stitching the patterns as she asked, "Grandfather, will you tell me what it is like when you walk into the other worlds?"

Drumming Deer continued his sewing as he answered her question:

"I think Spider Woman is happy that you are here with me and that you are asking this. Many winters ago, I visited the People of the Painted Earth Temple. Your Grandmother was a young woman at that time and we became friends. We shared the stories we had learned from our medicine teachers who live in different areas of Gaia's Land.

Spider Woman was very interested in the way I traveled into other worlds. You once described to me a feeling you experienced while dancing in your Harvest Moon ceremony. You said that your medicine animal, the bison, joined with you and shared your body as you danced. What you felt was the trail that leads to the door of the animal powers' world. You were taught by Spider Woman, and now you are the keeper of the mysteries she passed to you. Because of this, I will teach you how to walk through the doors into other worlds."

Drumming Deer set down his sewing and picked up his drum. He had White Bison Calf sit cross-legged with her back straight and her hands relaxed in her lap. She recognized this as the position for meditation that Grandmother Spider Woman had taught to her.

Deer beat his drum as he spoke to her. "Think of a time when you had a special encounter with a crow. Remember how this bird moved and imagine how the crow felt as it moved. Holding your intention to go there, think of a place to which you would like to travel. Feel the crow enter into your body and become one with you. Listen to the drum, relax, and allow yourself to leave your body here with me while flying off within the crow's body. After you have traveled to your destination, continue to follow the sound of my drum and return here to your body."

As Deer talked, he continued his rhythmic drumming. Calf could feel the crow medicine, although she also felt a little twinge of fear in her stomach about traveling as Deer had described. She slowly relaxed the tension in every part of her body. There was a popping sound, and her vision changed. She had left the world of color and solid things. Calf took a few hops on her crow's feet and cocked her head toward Drumming Deer. He looked amazing in this colorless world. Then Calf remembered the place she wanted to go.

Spreading her wings, she flew through the skins of Deer's tent into the winter sky. Calf was so thrilled to be flying that she experimented with dips, turns, and dives. She made ready to do another soaring dive in the gusty wind when she forgot about the drumming. The crow fell like a rock through the skins of Deer's tent. As it did so, the crow turned into Calf, who tumbled onto the floor in a heap.

Drumming Deer howled with laughter. When he could talk, he said, "That was pretty good, but next time do not forget to hold the sound of the drumbeat in your mind, even when your mind sees your destination. You must split your mind between the two as you enter the crow's body. This skill sometimes takes practice, but I believe you are closer to doing it than you think. Your experience of merging with the bison during the Harvest Moon Ceremony tells me this. You must release yourself to the powers within you, and trust them. Focus your mind on the drumbeat and keep it there. As you do, you will see where you want to go, and at that moment you will become the crow."

Placing herself again in her meditation position, Calf followed the drumbeat and Deer's instructions. She became a crow quickly and again flew through the tent into the sky. As she flew north she went faster and faster. The winter landscape below her became a blur of movement. Soon the forest disappeared and the world was all ice and snow.

The Frozen Lands ended and she was over a forest again. As she flew, the world changed to spring, and then to summer.

White Bison Calf found herself in a desert land with flat-topped mountains. She flew to a strange-looking village and entered a cave-like room under the ground. Spirit dancers with masks of ancestors and animal powers sat chanting in a circle. One of the dancers was Spotted Cat and she landed in front of him. She cocked her head and their eyes met. Following the instant of recognition between them, she again heard rhythmic drumming. The moment she focused on the drumbeat, she found herself sitting in her body looking at Drumming Deer in the world of color.

Calf exclaimed, "I saw Spotted Cat sitting in ceremony on Turtle Island!"

Deer chuckled at her.

"The way you just traveled, very few people have experienced. Before the Earth changes happened, many shamans and priestesses could walk between the worlds. Perhaps it is for the best that now only a few can still do this.

Our world is now full of strife and war and it is possible to use this power to harm other humans. To use the power from other worlds to harm the Slave Tribes would bring about a great disruption in the Sacred Balance. Many ages ago, this power was used wrongly and helped to bring about the Earth changes. Be very careful when using this teaching that I have given to you. Remember, use it only for healing and for gaining knowledge in the other worlds."

Deer put the last stitches on the boots as Calf asked, "How do you heal with this power?"

Drumming Deer answered, "If you had an illness that could not be healed, and the illness could not live in a crow's body, you could become a crow until the sickness was gone and then return to your body, which would now be free of it."

Deer then said to Calf, "Before winter is over we will leave for Turtle Island." Calf's eyes went wide with excitement. "Yes, I will be accompanying you through the Frozen Lands. I will set you on the right trail to Turtle Island before we part. Here, you will be needing these." Deer handed Calf the beautiful fur-lined boots he had been working on. Calf's heart filled with joy.

Before the next moon cycle ended, they prepared for the journey. The villagers piled many furs and food supplies in a huge basket. Attached to the bottom of the basket were two poles that curled up on the front end. Drumming Deer started to beat on his drum. Soon they heard hoof beats and eight reindeer came to him. They allowed Deer to tie the rope from the basket to their chests. Calf and Deer climbed into the basket and snuggled into the furs. While the tribe's people waved farewell, the drum spoke again and the reindeer broke into a run heading north, pulling behind them the priestess and the shaman.

Riding in a slides-along-in-the-snow basket behind the running reindeer was the most exhilarating thing Calf had ever experienced. They traveled like this for many days. The days turned into many moon cycles. Sometimes it seemed that they were in a dream, and soon Calf was not sure how many moons had passed. Behind them spring had come to the People of the Reindeer, even though Calf and Deer were in the land of forever winter. As they traveled north, the days became longer until the light stayed all day. Deer said that night did not come to the Frozen Lands during the Summer. He explained that they were crossing over the top of the Earth and soon they would be traveling south.

As they eventually headed south, the ice lands looked the same day after day and Calf lost all sense of the moon cycles. At last, patches of earth began to show through the endless snow. They entered a forest again as they traveled deeper into the lands of Turtle Island. The weather became milder as they went south, and it felt like they were traveling into spring. It could not be too many days until the snow would end.

As the snow became thinner Drumming Deer spoke to Calf. "White Bison Calf, soon I will put you upon the right trail. It is your destiny to go south until your heart says you have arrived at your new home. It is time for me to return to the People of the White Reindeer. The first village that you will visit is occupied by the People of the Salmon."

Deer talked for many days about the trails Calf would be walking on. When the snow became too thin for the reindeer basket, Deer stopped and said farewell. "Remember, White Bison Calf, you are the High Priestess of Gaia's Land and Spider Woman has sent you to this land with an important gift. Follow your heart and you will find the place of your Grandmother's dreams."

Once again, Calf saddened at having to say farewell to another friend and wise teacher. Yet her spirits rose as she realized that she was getting closer to fulfilling her lifelong destiny and finding her sacred reflection, Spotted Cat.

Chapter 13

The Sacred Pipe

After leaving Drumming Deer, Calf traveled through a dense forest with high mountains to the east. Much of the animal life was similar to Gaia's Land, and there were whole new families of animals as well. Some of the birds that Calf recognized had markings unlike the ones at home. Being in a new land excited her and she especially liked all the new bird songs.

After many days of walking in this beautiful forest, Calf began to see signs that people were near. Soon, she saw the village that Drumming Deer had described.

White Bison Calf's arrival caused a lot of excitement in the village. A lone woman had never walked down from the Frozen Lands before. In celebration of the traveler from the other side of the Earth, the villagers prepared a feast.

The People of the Salmon looked different from the other tribes she had encountered. They seemed to be a mixture of all peoples, including her tribe. A village of tents similar to the Reindeer People's homes spread near a very wide river. The villagers fished for large salmon with spears. Salmon meat dried on racks of sticks placed around campfires. The smoked salmon at the feast was the best meat she had ever tasted.

After they could eat no more, the villagers reclined and relaxed. Soon they took out objects they called pipes. They put herbs into the pipes and then lit them with fire. The tribal members would then draw the smoke from the burning herbs into their mouths and blow it into the air. The People of the Salmon seemed to enjoy the pipes, and the smoke coming out of their mouths fascinated Calf.

As Calf listened to the stories around the fire, she became sleepy and curled up in her sleeping furs, then drifted into a dream. A gigantic spider, much larger than herself, crept up to where she lay sleeping. She tried to struggle awake and run from it but felt paralyzed and could not move. The spider moved closer and, after a terrorizing moment of stillness, pounced on top of her. The giant spider started spinning her around and covering her in a web, as she had often watched spiders do to insects. The spider would then sting its prey to death.

White Bison Calf felt tightly wrapped in a bundle like a caterpillar in a cocoon. She mustered all her will to struggle against this confinement and finally burst the spiderweb bundle open. She crawled out and found butterfly wings attached to her back. Her wings were all crumpled and she was unable to fly as the spider hovered over her. Calf stared at the spider's large round abdomen and realized it was Grandmother Spider Woman's stomach she was looking at. The spider slowly transformed into her Grandmother. Spider Woman was sitting in ceremony, meditating. The sun rose during her morning ceremony and she smoked a pipe the way the Salmon People had by the campfire the night before. The smoke made her breath visible as it curled around toward the sunrise. As Spider Woman breathed out her prayers of thanksgiving to the sun, they became manifest.

The sun warmed White Bison Calf's wings and soon she knew she could fly. Calf flew into the sky, looking down upon Grandmother Spider Woman. The smoke from Grandmother's pipe now drifted toward the four directions. It formed a Sacred Cross like the first two strands of the web woven by First Woman. In the creation story, these two strands brought together the powers of the Four Grandparents of the All That Is. The luminous thread then traveled in a spiral of medicine energy with Spider Woman in the center. Just as the First Priestess in the creation story had done, Grandmother wove the smoke like strands of a great, luminous spider web. The prayers made visible in the pipe smoke reflected the teachings of the Web of Life. The smoke from Grandmother's Sacred Pipe now surrounded her in a visual manifestation of the teaching that Grandmother had given over the years to White Bison Calf.

Calf awoke from her vivid dream feeling both excited and refreshed. Although she didn't know why, she also felt more certain about, and more keenly focused upon, the destiny that Grandmother Spider Woman had so clearly imparted to her in the dream.

After several days of rest, Calf joined a group of hunters heading south to hunt buffalo. As a parting gift, the villagers gave her a white deerskin dress with long, flowing fringe. It was decorated with many colored quills from one of the animals that lived in the forest. They also gave her one of their pipes in a beautifully decorated deerskin bag. Calf was not sure what she would do with this pipe but she felt it would be wrong to refuse the gift.

As the hunters walked south, they kept the mountain range toward the sunrise. After a crescent-to-full moon cycle, they turned on to a mountain pass. In the mountains, autumn colors painted the trees. As they descended into a river valley, it still felt like summer.

The travelers soon began to see signs of buffalo. The hunters became very excited at the first sight of one. It was similar to the bison of Gaia's Land, except that it was smaller and shaggier. The group divided when they came to a large valley heading south. The hunters continued east, and Calf walked alone toward the valley.

The next day, Calf came upon a large herd of buffalo. She felt as if she was getting close to the doorway between the worlds as she approached her power animal. As she walked toward the herd, she could feel herself beginning to enter the spirit world. But before she did, she saw two young men approaching her. One of the men broke away from the other and ran toward her. He was very muscular and handsome. She could feel a strong physical passion emanating from him, and she also felt something begin to stir within her own body that she had not felt for a long time. It had been many winters since she and Spotted Cat had touched each other by the singing stream. As the young man reached out for her, Calf heard a popping sound and knew that they had entered together into another world. It was a beautiful, lush world and they found themselves in a happy, friendly village next to a river where children played.

The young man, whose name was Eagle, wanted very much to mate with Calf. She realized that she would very much like to live in this peaceful village, so she allowed their physical joining to happen. Calf's awareness of her other life seemed to sink below her thoughts as she and Eagle gave love medicine to each other. She lost all sense of time.

Calf and Eagle's life together was very full and loving, and they raised two strong children. After many abundant winters, Eagle had become an old man, but White Bison Calf remained the same age as when she entered into this other world. Their children were all grown when Eagle died.

Calf took out her drum to sing a song over Eagle after he crossed over into the World of Spirit. As she beat the drum, she remembered Drumming Deer, and then she remembered Spotted Cat. She heard the strange sound of the door closing to the other world, and was suddenly back on Turtle Island. She stood facing Owl, the young man she had seen with Eagle, who was now staring in stunned surprise at Eagle's withered bones lying at Calf's feet.

White Bison Calf tried to explain to Owl what had just occurred, but she was very confused and disoriented and did not really understand herself much of what had happened. However, she hoped that Owl understood some of what she tried to say, and she also hoped that she had not wrongfully used the teachings of Drumming Deer. Even though his brother had disappeared, Owl seemed to grasp that something larger than life as he knew it had happened. He and Calf spoke for a while, and Calf explained who she was and the reason for her journey. Owl responded by telling Calf that he was the apprentice of a medicine woman in his tribe, Eyes of Wisdom. Calf soon realized that Owl was a sensitive man of spirit, and this made her feel a little more relieved about what had happened, although she still did not fully grasp it.

Calf felt a need to give a medicine gift to Owl. She thought about the pipe she now held in her hand and also about her dream of Spider Woman smoking it. Calf realized instantly that this might be a good way to begin imparting her message about the Web of Life. She knew that into this common object of Turtle Island's people could be woven a ceremony to express the Web's teachings. She said to Owl, "Go to your village and prepare a ceremonial lodge and I will bring a sacred gift to your people."

Owl had described to Calf his village and the powerful medicine woman to whom he was apprenticed. Later, when Calf walked to Owl's village, she went directly to the lodge of his medicine teacher, Eyes of Wisdom. Calf told this old medicine woman about her time in Gaia's Land, about her travels, and about her otherworld encounter with Eagle. Calf also told Grandmother about the gift of the Sacred Pipe Ceremony that she wished to give to the tribe.

Eyes of Wisdom looked thoughtful as she spoke to Calf:

"The wisdom of the Web of Life from your land, joining with the pipe from our land, sounds like good medicine. As for your time with my grandson, I feel your heart was in a good place when you and Eagle entered the other world. You should not worry about your joining with him. Yet, as your teacher Drumming Deer cautioned, you should be careful and have a clear intention and direction as you enter these other worlds.

You will be happy to know that a young man came to our village several winters ago and told of traveling from another land. His name was Spotted Cat and I am sure that he was the young man in your story. I told

148

him about my teacher in the Land of the Lying Down Mountains. After staying a while with us, he continued on his way south toward their village."

Calf felt like Eyes of Wisdom had just removed a very heavy load from her back, and she also knew that she must soon be on her way.

Calf's new Grandmother then told her about the tribe's stories and described their ceremonies. When she was finished, Eyes of Wisdom called Owl to her lodge and asked him to gather together a council meeting on the approaching day of the Autumn Equinox.

When the day after the sacred gift arrived, Calf and Eyes of Wisdom walked to the communal lodge in the center of the village. Inside it, eight medicine people sat in a circle in the middle of the gathered tribe. White Bison Calf sat in the circle and took out the pipe from the decorated pipe bag. She looked radiant as she began the ceremony, and the People sat in reverent stillness.

She lifted the bowl to the stem and said, "In celebration of All My Relations," and joined the two together. Speaking over the pipe, she continued:

"This pipe is to be your altar and a way to gather all the Powers of the Universe.

149

When you breathe out the smoke, it takes your prayers to All That Is. The pipe's bowl is in the shape of the feminine powers, and the stem is of the masculine powers. As the two are joined, there is a perfect balance, the balance we will all become as we join these two powers in our inner selves. When we place the tobacco into the pipe, we honor each power, starting with the Mother Earth and the Great Spirit. Then we invite the Grandparents of the east to come to the altar, the Helpers who come from the South, the Ones who come to us from the west, and the Spirits from the north. There is tobacco for the Sacred Tree that is in the center of our wheel when we Sundance, and for the Rainbow Powers that surround us with their protection. When the World of Plants is called to our ceremony, they bring all their gifts: herbs, food, fiber, and learning from our ancient teachers, the Trees. We honor all the Medicine Animals, each with its own special power that it brings to our circle. We invite our Ancestors, the Spirits, and the Teachers of all the Worlds that have something to teach us, or have something to help us with in our ceremony.

Before we light the fire to the tobacco and smoke, we again honor the Powers of the six directions by offering the pipe to them first: the Earth, the Sky, and the Grandparents of the four directions. When a man is praying with the pipe, the ceremony is the same except that he offers his prayers first to the Great Spirit and then to Mother Earth. This is to honor his place of origin on the Sacred Circle. As we smoke the Sacred Pipe, we offer into it our prayers for healing, peace, and understanding our place on the Wheel of Life. With this smoke, we send our voices to the Universe, and this smoke takes our prayers to our Helpers in the Sky and in the Earth."

At the end of the Sacred Pipe ceremony, White Bison Calf held the pipe above her head. Then she separated the bowl from the stem and said, "In celebration of All The People."

After the ceremony, Calf said farewell to her new friends and walked south along the trails that her new Grandmother had described to her. She understood that she still had a long walk ahead to find Spotted Cat, although in thinking about him and the eventual joyous end of her journey, her heart was light. Calf walked onto a wonderful, expansive grassland and felt an almost overwhelming sense of love. She came upon a herd of buffalo, and at the center of the herd she saw a small calf.

Remembering the dream she had during her initiation ceremony in the Painted Earth Temple, she walked toward the middle of the herd. The High Priestess of Gaia knew that she was again approaching the door between the worlds. Calf was drawn to the Grandmother Chief of the herd. Calf felt her energy begin to glow, first with all the colors, then becoming white as she merged with this wise elder. She felt her thoughts expand into the collective mind of the buffalo herd. Calf could sense the herd's need to migrate to more abundant pastures. She started walking toward greener fields and the whole herd followed. Calf was comforted to again be a part of a tribal community. She rejoiced that, for a while at least, she would have company on her journey.

The ceremony of the Sacred Pipe had moved Owl to follow the Gaia Priestess. Thinking about all the medicine teachings she had gifted to him during her stay with his tribe, his heart felt full. He thought at first that he was making sure that Calf went safely onto the correct path, but soon realized that he followed her because he didn't want to see her go.

Owl watched in awe as Calf started to glow and then transformed into a white buffalo. It left no doubt about what he had already envisioned—that she was a medicine woman of great power and wisdom. Owl felt that finding this new teacher was a sign that he should follow his own desire to become a tribal shaman. He pledged in his heart to follow the teachings of the Sacred Pipe on his way to doing this. Owl watched from a hilltop as the white buffalo led the herd slowly toward the south. In the bright sun, all the colors of the rainbow shimmered on her white fur. The luminance seemed to radiate from White Buffalo Woman throughout the entire Web of Life.

HO

List of Illustrations

I have included the pictures of my artwork in *Painted Earth Temple* so that the reader can feel the wisdom of the archetypal mythology through images as well as through literature. *These symbols speak not only to our minds but to a deeper part of us. They speak to us as our dreams speak to us.*

Good Medicine, Heyoka.

Page xii

"Creative Spiral." Spirals appear the world over and are among the oldest and most sacred of symbols. The design in this necklace is called Rain Bird Shield and is a Hopi symbol of the creative spiral. It is the spiral movement of creation incorporating all the elements that bring forth life. This spiral is reflected throughout nature, including the spiral molecules of DNA, the building blocks of life.

Page xvi

"Spider Woman." To the Pueblo Indians, Spider Woman is the Creator of the Universe. She began by spinning two threads, east-west and north-south. She produced two daughters who made the Sun and Moon. She made the people from yellow, red, black, and white clay. In Europe she was called Athene, spinner of fate who bore the name of Arachne in a spider incarnation.

Page 12

"Sky Mother." Sky Mother is the Sacred Void that existed before the manifest universe. The lightning bolts are the first spirit (Sky Father) flashing through the blackness of the Sacred Void.

Page 22

"Crow Mother."

Rhea Kronia, Mother Crow
    Holding together time and space
Wisdom Woman, nurturing Earth
    Giving teacher, Grandmother Crone
Angwusnasomtaka, Crow Mother
    Kachina of initiation
Singing Valkrie, angels flying
    Bring our souls to spirit realms
Sacred Crow, eldest ancestor
    Watching generations come and go

Page 36

"Sky Father." The first spirit was called Sky Father. To the Native Americans, the eagle symbolizes spirit. The bird-man portrayed in this sculpture is an archetypal image that appears in many different cultures. As Sky Father touches the shield of life, the one spirit becomes many spirits.

Page 42

"**Tree Spirit.**" Many people have a view of Nature that each tree, plant, or flower has a spirit living within it. This spirit is the consciousness that sleeps within the seed and guides the growth of the plant throughout its life. A tree spirit is called a Dryad.

Page 54

"**Dragon Birds.**" It is easy to see why swans were chosen to be the keepers of the dreamtime. When we see a swan gliding upon the mirror of a still pond, we are easily carried into a quiet, dreamy receptivity. Swans also symbolized the Muses who brought, through artists, inspiration from the dream world. Another name for swans is Freya's Dragons.

Page 64

"**Earth Father.**" One of the names of the first man on earth was Earth Father. In the Southwest of the United States he is called Thundering Earth, and he is the archetypal Horned God that is found in many cultures. The Horned God dances a circle of protection around the First Mother. Without him to guard her, the Earth Mother would not have a protected place in which to work her magic of birthing.

Page 76

"Goddess of the White Horse." On a green hillside near Uffington, England, there is a 370-foot chalk-cut image of the White Mare. Epona, goddess of the white horse, was honored all over Europe. The Mare Goddess was the title applied to the queen of the Amazons, the goddess-worshiping tribes that held influence from North Africa to Northern Europe.

Page 88

"Rainbow Bison." The rainbow and the white bison are powerful archetypes both in the Old World and the New. On Turtle Island, this energy is said to bring the unification of the black, red, white, and yellow races. In the old prophecies this new tribe is called the Rainbow Tribe or the Warriors of the Rainbow.

Page 108

"Gaia's Temple." The Goddess within the shrine is Gaia, which is the ancient Greek name for Mother Earth. They called her the Oldest of Divinities. Gaia's most ancient temples were in caves that were sometimes painted with animal and human deities.

Page 118

"White Bison Calf." In Europe, the white bison is a sign of great hope, much as the white buffalo is to the peoples of the New Lands. To many Native Americans, it means the return of the power of White Buffalo Woman, bringing healing to Mother Earth.

Page 130

"Shaman." The first man on Earth was also the first shaman. He taught that all animals were related to our human family. Every encounter with an animal was a gift from the animal powers. In mythical symbolism, the shaman is like the Horned God or Father Earth that is found in cultures all over the world.

Page 140

"Earth Mother." White Buffalo Woman is the Native American archetype for the Earth Mother and she is depicted here blessing the world of Sky Father's spirits with the ceremonial pipe. As she prays over the shield of spirit, the animals awaken with physical life. The world is now both spirit and substance animated with the breath of life.

Page 154

"White Buffalo Woman." Long ago, two young men were crossing the plains in the center of the land they called Turtle Island, which we now have named America. They saw a person approaching them from a distance, and soon they could see a beautiful woman dressed in white buckskin. She came holding the pipe in her hands. She taught them to honor everything in the universe when tobacco is put into the pipe. The pipe was to be an altar and the center of their ceremonies. As the woman walked away, she turned into a white buffalo.

To view more of Heyoka Merrifield's artwork, visit his website at www.heyoka-art.com.

Cover art by Keith Powell at www.powellartstudio.com

Printed in the United States
By Bookmasters